YA Taylor
Taylor, Cora
Finding Melissa

$12.95
ocn869776721
07/25/2014

finding
melissa

WITHDRAWN

finding melissa

Cora Taylor

Fitzhenry & Whiteside

Text copyright © 2014 Cora Taylor

Published in Canada by Fitzhenry & Whiteside,
195 Allstate Parkway, Markham, Ontario L3R 4T8

Published in the United States by Fitzhenry & Whiteside,
311 Washington Street, Brighton, Massachusetts 02135

All rights reserved. No part of this book may be reproduced
in any manner without the express written consent of the publisher,
except in the case of brief excerpts in critical reviews and articles.
All inquiries should be addressed to Fitzhenry & Whiteside Limited,
195 Allstate Parkway, Markham, Ontario L3R 4T8.

www.fitzhenry.ca   godwit@fitzhenry.ca
10 9 8 7 6 5 4 3 2 1

Library and Archives Canada Cataloguing in Publication
Finding Melissa
ISBN 978-1-55455-274-0 (Paperback)
Data available on file

Publisher Cataloging-in-Publication Data (U.S.)
Finding Melissa
ISBN 978-1-55455-274-0 (Paperback)
Data available on file

Fitzhenry & Whiteside acknowledges with thanks the Canada Council for the
Arts, and the Ontario Arts Council for their support of our publishing program.
We acknowledge the financial support of the Government of Canada through
the Canada Book Fund (CBF) for our publishing activities.

Cover and interior design by Tanya Montini
Cover image courtesy of Debi Bishop/Getty Images
Printed in Canada

To my Grandson,
Justin Livingston.
Alexander — you'll get the next one!

* * *

Thank you to fellow author Janice MacDonald
for reading the ms. way back when I first wrote it,
and for her encouragement. And to my Agent,
Lynn Bennett at Transatlantic Literary Agency,
for her belief that this book should be published.
I'm grateful to the students of Tomahawk School
for helping me with names. And most of all
to my husband, Earl Georgas, for his love
and support when I needed it.

On Sunday, two-and a-half-year-old Melissa Warren disappeared while her parents, Arthur and Joanne Warren were tenting at the North Thompson River Campground north of Blue River, British Columbia. Search parties failed to locate any trace of the little girl in the dense bush around the campground. Proximity to the river raised the possibility that she had been swept away by the rushing water, still high from spring runoff and flooding.

"She'd sometimes wake up before the rest of us," her distraught mother explained, "but we were careful to put her in the back of the tent... she had to climb over the rest of us in our sleeping bags. I don't know how she got out. When we woke up she wasn't there!"

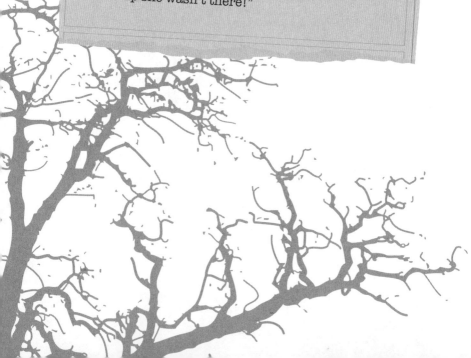

Search parties continue to comb the forest around the North Thompson River Campground in Northern B.C. where two-year-old Melissa Warren disappeared on Sunday but no trace of the Vancouver girl has been found. Attempts to drag the North Thompson River failed to recover a body.

The family dog, a border collie-terrier cross, had left the tent as well. It was found dead under some nearby brush with several wounds including slashes to its throat. Sightings of a sow grizzly in the area caused speculation that the child had been carried off by a bear.

The Warrens, who are from North Vancouver, have one other child, five-year-old Clarice, who had accompanied them on the camping holiday.

NEWSPAPER CLIPPING - June 25, 1990

RCMP have called off the search for the Vancouver two-year-old who disappeared near the North Thompson River although the Missing Child Alert is still in place.

chapter one

Private Journal of Clarice Warren
June 14, 2012

So the new guidance counsellor at school thinks the reason I get in trouble so much is Guilt. Ms. Madison, fresh out of some stupid Education Psych course, found out about my "missing sister" story and dredged the whole thing up again. I'm supposed to "talk it out." Find out why I don't get along at school. I didn't tell her I get along way better there than I do at home—living with a mother who hates the sight of me.

So here I am, not "talking it out" (no way I'm going to do that and I told her so). I'm supposed to "write it out." Do the Journal Thing and write about it. Teachers are mad about journals these days. Only in this case Madison says it can be private. She says I don't have to show it to anyone, so I could just forget it and say I did…but what the hell. I might as well. It'll be a good way to vent. Nobody else to talk to.

Or I could just rant on and on about my mother. How many years did I try to please her? Too many. Then in high school I learned that getting into trouble gets you noticed and it's way easier than getting straight-A report cards. But my mother never seemed to care. Just looked at me with that look. As if I was only fulfilling something she'd known all along. I was *not* the Good Daughter. The Good Daughter was gone. Being the perfect little girl for Mummy didn't work. There was always the tragic, lost, little girl. Darling Melissa.

Not gone. Lost. Being lost means that she *could* be found. Technically. And my mother has never given up. Never stopped believing that somewhere, someday, Melissa will show up.

She gets this artist from Child Find to do portraits of Melissa-as-she-would-be each year. There is a line of them hanging on her bedroom wall. Except the current one. It's in a fancy frame in the living room. Melissa at fourteen. The artist has made her hair long. She looks a bit like Hilary Duff. Actually she looks *a lot* like Hilary Duff. As if that fat little rug rat would have turned out looking that good. I think the artist realizes he's onto a good thing. My mother pays him big bucks to turn the regular sketches into oil paintings suitable for framing. And mooning over.

There are *no* portraits of me in the house. Just the usual school photos that get done every year, tucked in Dollarama frames in the bedroom. Last fall, I didn't bother to pick mine up and bring it home. She never noticed.

But we've got this fancy portrait in the living room. Portrait of a Dead Kid, I call it.

After Dad moved out, I thought maybe he and I could have some sort of life. Something that wasn't haunted by Melissa.

Mum never shut up about her and so I thought Dad was just going along with it. I heard him arguing with Mum once. "We might just have to accept that she drowned. She's gone. We have to get on with our lives…"

Sitting here with my laptop, that's what I remember most about Melissa's disappearance. A huge hurt inside. Like the whole world had somehow twisted around and I was left. Alone. Not just without a sister—without a mother, too.

I must have been eight or nine by then. Mum had been so wrapped up in all the posters and work she was doing with Child Find—she practically ran the local branch of it—that it was her whole life. I remember the screaming when he said that. He shut up in a hurry and never said anything like it again but she never forgave him, hardly ever spoke to him after that. And he left soon after.

In the last few years, I thought of saying something like that myself. Shock treatment. "Hey, lady…your kid's been eaten by a bear…get over it!" But I never had the nerve.

So Ms. Madison thinks I'm 'acting up' because of Melissa's disappearance. I'm supposed to be carrying some kind of "baggage." When you've been questioned from the time you were five, over and over again, about something that just seemed like a bad dream at the time, the last thing you want to do is "talk it out." So it's, "Hello, journal."

Melissa was two. I'd just had my fifth birthday. I remember the morning. Waking up to the screaming.

It was cold. I remember just wanting to snuggle down in my sleeping bag and go back to sleep like I'd done before. But Mum was grabbing me, pulling me out. So I was standing outside the tent, shivering in my Minnie Mouse PJs. The sun was hitting the tent and drops of water caught the light, making tiny sparkles all over it. I was in my bare feet on the cold ground. Sharp pine needles jabbing my toes. I was jumping up and down. Maybe I wanted to pee. And Mum was shaking me. Screeching.

"Where is she? Didn't you feel her crawl over you?"

Then she sort of calmed down. "Think, Clarice! Did you see the baby get up?"

I remember saying, "Maybe she's with Daddy." I couldn't see Dad either so it seemed obvious. I used to try to tell her something that might be true. She obviously wanted an answer so I'd try to think of something. It took me a while to learn that she considered that lying. I hadn't learned yet that if you hadn't seen it, you weren't supposed to speculate.

She started shaking me again, crying real loud. "He's looking for her!"

There was only one other family at the campground. They were in one of those camper trucks and now I could see the man climbing out and my mother ran over to him asking if he'd seen Melissa. I was glad she left me alone. I was going to go back in the tent to my comfy sleeping bag but I think the sun was warmer now.

Anyway, I thought I'd better go look for Melissa, too. The night before, we'd been playing while Dad made hot dogs for our supper. I'd found a neat place to play house when we first arrived.

There was a spruce tree near the edge of the campground and the branches came right down to the ground. Under the circle of branches it was like a cosy cave. Big enough for me to hide. But our dog, Lucky, found me, and Melissa had been following him so she crawled in, too. I let her stay because I knew if I chased her out she'd howl and I'd get yelled at. I was going to go get a blanket and make it all comfy but then it was time for supper. We had a campfire and I got to roast my own marshmallow after and Melissa didn't. And then we had to go to bed.

So the first place I looked was there, in our little hidey-hole. That's why I was the one who found Lucky. I didn't know he was dead but I knew by the blood that he had a major owie. So I stayed there holding him.

I could hear Dad's voice.

"Where's Clarice?" he was yelling. "Don't tell me you've let her wander off, too!"

And Mum, in scream mode again. "Did you find her? Did you find Melissa?" And Dad yelling my name, so I left Lucky and crawled out. I was crying and I must have had a lot of blood on me. I remember Mum screeching again and running toward me and I thought she was running to me because she thought I was hurt so I held out my arms. But she just knocked me down. She ran right by with Dad on the other side of her. He got there first and pulled away the branches.

And I just sat there looking after my mother, knowing something I'd maybe only suspected before: I didn't matter.

Somebody must have called the Mounties because there were cars with flashing lights that I thought were very pretty once the howl of the sirens stopped.

Someone I didn't know picked me up and bundled me into a blanket and put me on the picnic table bench. I could see a policeman putting Lucky in his car.

I wanted to go and stop him but I was afraid Mum would scream at me again. And I didn't want the policemen to notice me and ask me questions but they did anyway.

Nicer than my mother though. The one who questioned me squatted down by the picnic table and spoke very quietly in a friendly voice.

"You must be Clarice," he said.

I think I nodded.

"We're going to look for your little sister for you."

I doubt if I nodded at that. At that point I didn't much care if they found her or not. She wasn't much fun to play with and she was always getting into my things. Taking stuff. And when I'd take it back she'd bawl and get me in trouble. I guess in my kid mind, I thought she was the reason my mother hated me.

"Do you remember what happened?"

"Melissa's gone," I said.

"Was she gone when you woke up this morning?"

"Yes," I said. Then he went away and I sat there while the lady from the camper brought me a cookie and a plastic glass full of milk. I remember that part because my mother never filled the glass full but the lady did, as if she thought I was big enough not to spill. So I was very careful and didn't.

The man in the camper said he'd heard something but thought someone was coming to camp and didn't bother to look out.

I guess that was what made my mother believe Melissa had been kidnapped. But we were so close to the river. My Dad said that he thought Lucky'd come back to die under the tree because they found blood by the river. And then everybody started talking about a grizzly bear near there.

For years my mother blamed the police. After my dad and me, of course. She always said that they should have checked for tire tracks before all those people came for the search party.

In the beginning, Dad would explain that they'd checked for cars going through the Jasper Park entrance but it was no use. She was sure that Melissa was out there and they could find her if they really tried.

I volunteered at the Child Find office one summer while I was still trying to be The Good Daughter. There was another lady helping in the office, and when Mum was out one afternoon I asked her the big question.

"How many of these 'kidnapped' children ever turn up alive? I mean, what are the statistics?"

She just sighed. "Don't tell your mother I told you, but after more than ten years? I've never heard of even one." Right away she seemed to regret having said that. "Promise you won't say anything. I think hope is all that keeps your mother going."

I promised. By then I knew there was no point in anybody trying to tell my mother anything. In that regard she was hope-less.

chapter two

Leesa

There's a recurring dream I've had ever since I can remember. I am in a beautiful world of green with flickering lights shining through. Not alone. There is something soft to cuddle with. Maybe it's a teddy bear.

Strange. The dream, except for the colour and flashes of light, is strongest by the smell and feel of it. A prickly feeling as I lie holding the softness. There is green close above. It has a sharp, clean smell. We are hiding there and the green keeps us safe.

Then everything changes. The softness is gone. Snatched away. And the sharp, clean smell of green is gone, too. Something is coming at me. I try to get away but there is no place to go and I am scared and I can't scream because I can't breathe. A dirty, slippery-feeling yellow cloth is over my face. There's a sweet, sick smell. And then the dream is over.

I have other dreams now and then, but they are just

fragments. People I don't know and a strange house. The clearest part of that dream is a doll house with tiny perfect furniture that a big girl who is my sister—I don't really have a sister—won't let me play with. I take a little rocking chair and put it in my pocket and she doesn't know. It is a perfect replica of an old-fashioned rocker. It even has a tiny cushion, red with gold trim.

Now that I am older, I hardly ever have those dreams. But I do have nightmares. These are real and they belong to the time before I came to live with Aunt Rosie when I was very little. I try not to think about them. When I was younger I would wake up screaming. Now I just wake up in a cold sweat afraid to move or open my eyes.

I woke up screaming again last night. The first time I've done that for months, maybe years. When it happened before, I'd lie in my bed, feet tangled in the covers, and wait for Aunt Rosie to come. She always comes. Always holds me the way she did when I was little.

And she always says the same thing: "There, there, my pet." Over and over. Sometimes when I finally stop shaking and look up at her, there are tears in her eyes.

Last night was different. When the scream started it felt as if my throat closed, as if somehow I couldn't scream—mustn't scream. I lay there with my eyes shut tight. Awake but not awake. Stone still. Someone was coming and if I didn't move, didn't wake up, maybe whoever it was would go away.

But I must have screamed because Aunt Rosie came and when her hand touched my forehead I jumped away as if she had burned me. This time the feeling of terror was so strong it blocked out everything else. My whole body began to ache. I couldn't move—I could just lie there looking up at her.

"Poor pet. I was hoping you were over the night terrors." She sighed. "It's been a long time, nearly a year, isn't it? Maybe you're just worried. It is final exam time."

Somehow that snaps me out of it. I start to jump out of bed. Have I slept in? I can't see the clock on the dresser. But it is still dark, and June in northern Alberta would mean light coming in my window. The sun rises long before I have to.

Aunt Rosie pats my shoulder. "It's only 2 a.m. I don't suppose, though, that you'll be able to get back to sleep." Another sigh.

Poor Auntie, I think, and I give her a hug. "Sorry," I say. "Interrupting your sleep…must be just like having a baby in the house. Yelling for its two o'clock feeding!" I feel better now and just want to erase the tired, worried look on her face.

A small Mona Lisa sort of smile rewards the effort. "Well, of course, I didn't know you then." She gets up slowly. "Your mama would have had that job. You know I didn't get you until you were nearly three years old."

I know the story. At least, I know the parts Aunt Rosie has told me. My parents weren't married, weren't even living together, but my mother had decided she didn't want to be tied down with a kid and had hunted my dad down and left me with him. He was Auntie's only brother—much younger, a big age difference. Age-wise she's more like a grandmother to me. Anyway, he'd brought me here and dumped me on his sister.

Lucky for me. Maybe not-so-lucky for her.

But she never complained. And she loved me—loves me—I know that.

She isn't like the other kids' mothers, of course. Old-fashioned. I guess that was normal, living as she had before I came. The house is old. It had been her parents' and she kept it up as best she could. Once there'd been a whole section of land, but that had been sold off a quarter section at a time. She'd kept the home quarter as long as she could but finally sold it to a neighbour, just keeping the house, the yard, and four or five acres. I guess if we'd been closer to a big city it would be called an acreage. We keep a cow for milk and chickens for eggs—she sells the extra—there are regular customers every week. Aunt Rosie has a huge vegetable garden with half an acre in potatoes. She cans and freezes everything and keeps the potatoes down in the dirt-cellar.

Fetching the potatoes for Aunt Rosie has been my job since the time I was old enough to manage the steep steps down. All winter long, I'd lift up the cellar door in the middle of the kitchen floor and go down into the sharp darkness—past the shelves of canned tomatoes, fruit and berries, the jams and jellies, and pickled beets shining dimly in the light. Colours sparkling, the apricots like big orange eyes watching me. On to the dark potato bin that took up half of the cellar. If I forgot to take a flashlight, I'd just feel for the potatoes, gathering enough to fill the little pail I'd brought.

In early spring, the potato bin would have nearly emptied but far back in the darkest corner of the cellar would be the last few potatoes. White sprouts, like ghostly fingers, mushrooming up everywhere. When I was really little they made me cry and run back up the stairs.

We managed, Aunt Rosie and I. And ever since I was old enough, I've helped.

I never regretted losing my teenager mother. Good luck to her.

Sometimes, though, I wish my useless father would help Aunt Rosie out. Send some money for clothes for me. We are too far from any neighbours with small children for me to earn money babysitting.

That's going to change this summer. I have a job. I am going to be a live-in babysitter for the daughter-in-law of one of Auntie's friends. I just wish Auntie wouldn't keep saying I'm their "hired girl." Nobody calls it that anymore. That term went out with hooped skirts. On the other hand, nobody around Tomahawk, Alberta has got onto saying "*au pair* girl" yet either.

Whatever it's called. I'll be starting in less than two weeks. As soon as exams are over and school is out.

I try not to let on but I am plenty nervous. I'll be moving over to the Friesens' and the deal is that I'll have Sunday off but have to be back in time for Rhonda Friesen to go to work at the nursing home Monday morning.

The trouble is I don't know the Friesens all that well. Rhonda's husband's mother is a friend of Aunt Rosie's, a nice old-fashioned woman who gardens and knits and does Aunt Rosie stuff. I've known Bessie Friesen all my life. But I've only met Rhonda once or twice. Peter Friesen met her when he was working at the pulp mill in Hinton one winter. She seems okay but she smokes and drinks, so her mother-in-law doesn't approve. Though Bessie doesn't say anything right out, I can tell she doesn't really trust her son's wife much.

Maybe that's why I had the nightmare. The old recurring dream/scream stuff because I'm worried. And scared. For the first time in my life, I'll be leaving the warm safety of home and Aunt Rosie.

Well, not the first time because I guess I was with my mother and then my father but I don't remember anything "safe" before Aunt Rosie.

And I know I'm different.

Maybe it's because of being an only kid living here in the bush or maybe it's because of not being able to keep up with the other kids at school, clothes and other stuff-wise, but over the years I developed into a loner.

Or maybe I just prefer my own company. "Doesn't socialize well." Those words have been on my report cards since grade one. Although now that I'm in junior high, teachers have given up commenting on it. When you get mostly A's and B+'s they shouldn't complain.

chapter three

Heck hadn't been able to believe his luck when the two little girls came out of the tent. He'd had his eye on the oldest one for two days now.

He saw them first at a gas station restaurant in Merritt. The family was stopped, having a meal. Parents and two little girls—nothing special. But then the oldest one—five or six, maybe—nice little blond-curly-haired-type—had come running along just as he was leaving the Men's.

"Want some gum?" Heck said, sliding the package of Wrigley's out of his pocket. One stick slipped toward her. Tantalizing. He watched as she looked. He could see she was tempted but then she looked back toward the restaurant.

It was the smile she'd given him before she turned back to wait for her mother and sister that made him sit in his truck to watch the family as they got in their station wagon and headed out onto the highway. A smug smile. The kind of you-can't-have-me smile girls used to give him at home, before they learned better.

That smile made him follow, made him notice that they were turning north. Well, he was going north, too. Following gave him something to do. Gave the drive a bit of purpose other than just getting back to Alberta.

They'd stopped at the campground in Little Fort for the night and he'd decided to stop, too. There was a vacancy at the Wild Horse Motel. And he could afford it. He'd be getting paid damn good for hauling the stuff from Van.

He'd probably have forgotten all about them if he hadn't seen the station wagon pulling out of the Esso station when he pulled in to top off the tank before setting out next morning. The blond kid was looking out the window. At him. He was sure.

So why not catch up to them and follow again? Kind of fun.

They stopped for lunch in Blue River. So did he. This time he didn't go to the same restaurant but he sat at a table by the window across the way so he could see when they pulled out. It wasn't hard to catch up with them again.

He'd driven on past when they'd turned in at the campground. But then he got to thinking. Why not go back? He could park and sleep in the truck. He waited until it was good and dark. Only two vehicles at the campsite and the other one was a camper, so it wasn't hard to figure out that the tent was theirs. He was just about to pull into an empty spot when he saw the kids come out of the tent. The big one's hair was all fluffed up around her head, shining like some shampoo ad on TV. Bet it smelled nice, like some fruit or flower. Soft, too.

The little one and a dog were heading past the picnic bench toward the trees. But then the big one turned to go back into the tent. Heck was sure she'd call her sister to come, too. Maybe she did but the little one didn't pay any attention. Just kept going and disappeared under the branches of a big spruce tree. He hadn't parked yet, hadn't really pulled right into the camp. Maybe the littlest kid had just gone to get something. Maybe she'd head back to the tent right away. But she didn't. Maybe the big one would come out. But she didn't either.

He'd turned the truck so the lights were shining away from the two camping spots and dimly toward the tree the kid and dog were under. He was just curious, he told himself, but he took the chloroformed rag he always carried. It would keep the dog from barking. Those little dogs were yappy as hell.

Heck hadn't used it on the dog and he was driving through Hinton before the kid woke up, moaning. Then she'd puked all over the passenger seat. Just his luck. He cuffed her for it and she started howling. No way he could take her into a gas station washroom then, so he pulled off and got some water from the ditch and cleaned things up. Even so, he had to drive with the windows open because of the stink.

She was so little and she just sat there, tears coming down her cheeks, gasping like somebody'd knocked the wind out of her.

He was due back in Edmonton to drop off the load but he'd phone Stony and say he'd had car trouble. That should give him the little bit of extra time he needed.

He was going to have to make a detour. He'd head south at Entwistle and go to his sister's on the old farm place. Make up a story and dump the kid. Rosie might not believe him but she'd never turn the kid out.

By the time he got to Edson, the kid had cried herself to sleep so he could leave her in the truck while he checked into the motel. He got a unit in the back so nobody'd see him carrying her in. She didn't even wake up when he dumped her on the bed. He had to haul all the stuff in, too. It was in a couple of battered old suitcases so he figured that even if somebody saw him it wouldn't matter.

The kid woke up once but she shut up when he raised his hand. He was feeling high by then. Hoped Stony wouldn't be too pissed that he'd helped himself to a little of the stuff. Let him take it out of the payment.

By the time he was back on the road to Tomahawk, Heck had things figured out. A good story, too. He hadn't been back for four or five years so it could be true. It was even starting to look like a good idea—he could leave the kid with Rosie until she was older and then collect her again in a few years.

The kid was just sitting there, sort of crumpled up against the passenger door, whimpering.

"What's your name?" he asked her as friendly as he could.

She stopped snivelling and mumbled something.

"Ssseesa…"

Crap! It could be Sarah or Shauna or damn near anything. Could be Caesar for all he could tell. People gave their kids funny names these days. He'd have to work out something to tell Rosie.

chapter four

Private Journal of Clarice Warren

Writing this journal has made me really think about that night again. A lot. Stuff I hadn't thought about or wanted to think about for a long time.

And I think I remember something about that morning. Before the screaming. Before Melissa disappeared. I can't even write it down yet.

HOW DID I NOT REMEMBER THIS YEARS AGO?

It's a scary thing to figure that out after all this time. It makes my chest tighten and ache but I don't know what to do about it. Too late to tell anyone now, isn't it? It would just make Mum hate me more, wouldn't it?

This is what I remember:

The policeman at the picnic table that day hadn't asked me if I woke up in the night when Melissa did. Would I have told him that I followed her out? That I watched her follow Lucky over to the tree we'd played under before?

I didn't go with her—the needles were scratching my bare feet. Melissa had on her Dr. Denton sleepers—Extra Large for Chubbies—so her feet were okay.

So now, I'm beginning to wonder how I saw all this in the dark. Saw her go into the little hidey hole. I guess, at the time, the light didn't register in my five-year-old brain because it was about the same as when we'd gone to bed. Twilight. Long shadows stretching across the part between the tent and the tree.

Remembering it now, I know that there was light. It was shining through the trees. I realize now that there must have been a car parked in the trees at the entrance to the campground.

chapter five

Leesa

On Saturday night, I took my time packing for my first week at the Friesens' place.

Sorting, folding, tucking things neatly into my backpack. Toothbrush, toothpaste, make-up, panties, an extra pair of jeans, a couple of tops. I figured I wouldn't need much for now but I didn't want to forget anything. I knew if I did, I wouldn't be able to get back for it until Saturday night when Peter Friesen drove me home.

Aunt Rosie insisted that I come home then. "If you bring her Sunday morning and she has to be back Sunday night... that's not much of a day off, is it? She should have at least twenty-four hours. Last I heard, that was a day!"

Sometimes Aunt Rosie can be pretty spunky. That's her word, too. "It doesn't hurt to be 'spunky'," she says. "Stand up for yourself. If you don't, nobody else will!" Except I've got Aunt Rosie to stand up for me, too.

Bessie said Rhonda wasn't a bit happy about that arrangement. My getting Saturday night off. I was washing dishes while she and Aunt Rosie finished their tea but when I looked over, I could see Bessie was. Happy, that is. Anything that bugs Rhonda is alright with her. No love lost there.

That isn't exactly great with me. I would rather Rhonda didn't associate me with her mother-in-law. But since Bessie is Aunt Rosie's best friend there is no way I won't have a bit of a strike against me. The miracle is that I got the job at all. I'm sure it is Bessie's influence with her son that did it. Another reason for Rhonda to be hostile toward me. Just what I need.

Like I wasn't nervous enough already.

When Peter came to pick me up Aunt Rosie gave me a hug and whispered, "You can do it! Be my spunky girl!" I gave her a big smile, but on the inside my stomach was churning. If Aunt Rosie thinks I need spunk, she must believe that things won't go easy.

They don't.

Luckily, Rhonda is usually gone all day and the Friesen kids, Aggie and Dawson, are good kids most of the time. Aggie turned five last month and Dawson is just over a year. Aggie's real name is Agnetha after Bessie's mother. I already heard how Rhonda lost the battle naming her daughter although she'd managed to avoid having the little girl nicknamed "Netty" after the great-grandmother. A big loss on Bessie's part.

By the time the little boy Friesen was born, Rhonda had more say. Every time Bessie says, "Dawson," she rolls her eyes at the "newfangled" name. Usually she just refers to him as "Peter's boy" or "my grandson" since he's the only one she has.

Evenings are tough. I cook supper for everybody; but the kids and I have to eat first. Rhonda doesn't like the kids at the table when she and Peter eat. I don't think Peter likes this. He's crazy about his kids and sneaks in to play with them the minute supper is over. That's good for me as I'm free to clean up and do dishes. Which would be okay, except Rhonda is free too. Free to complain about the meal in some way although she told me what to cook and how to cook it before she left in the morning and I think I usually manage pretty well.

For the first few days Peter would say something like, "Good meal, Leesa," afterward but that always got him a dirty look from Rhonda so he stopped.

And then she always finds something to complain about with my housekeeping. A toy that strays outside the kids' rooms gives her an excuse to lecture. Heaven help me if I haven't folded the towels right when I do the laundry.

I'm dreading tomorrow: the first Saturday when Rhonda will be home all day. The only thing that makes me think I can stand it is knowing that after supper that night I can go home. As the week goes on I'm even more grateful to my spunky aunt.

This afternoon, Bessie drops by to see how I'm doing. The kids are all over her like fleas. They're beginning to like me but Bessie'd been their babysitter before me and besides, she's their grandmother.

It's great for me because it gives me time to get a head start on supper. Rhonda cut this recipe out of *Canadian Living* magazine but it calls for cumin and some other spices I can't find. Bessie's no help.

"Just tell Miss High-and-Mighty you only know how to make meatloaf!"

At least she whispers it so Aggie doesn't hear. I'm learning that Aggie's a lot smarter than her mother gives her credit for. Learning too that Rhonda definitely prefers her son to her daughter. Maybe it's the name but I can see Aggie's open, happy face shrivel a little when her mother comes home from work. Nobody has to tell her she has no right to keep whatever she's playing with if Dawson wants it. She just sits back and lets him take it. I guess the age difference could explain it, but I'm pretty sure she's figured out who really matters.

I'm not sure if it was that but I really knock myself out to make sure Aggie gets lots of attention when I'm able to give it. When Dawson takes his afternoon nap I try to do something special with her. We used to colour or cut out pictures for a little scrapbook I was helping her make. Things she can't do if Dawson is around because he'd eat the crayons or tear up the paper. We had to quit the scrapbook when Rhonda discovered we'd cut a picture out of one of her magazines.

"It was just an ad…there was nothing on the back…" I thought I'd try a little spunk. That was early in the week before I learned that it's better just to shut up and avoid Rhonda's snit fits.

Anyway, I make Bessie some tea and go to get Dawson up from his nap when Rhonda comes home from work an hour early. I can hear the "snit" hit the fan all the way upstairs.

Thank goodness Dawson has a messy diaper and it takes

me awhile to get him wiped up and changed. For once I'm grateful for the Gross! By the time we get downstairs, Bessie is gone. More or less thrown out of her son's house.

But Rhonda isn't finished. "What was *she* doing here?" She turns on me, her voice shrill. At the best of times Rhonda has a voice like barbed wire—single-strand barbed wire—thin but sharp and prickly; when she is riled it can slice you to ribbons. I can see Aggie huddled on the couch, pale and fighting back tears.

For once I don't back down. Maybe Aunt Rosie is channelling "spunk" at me.

"I'm just the hired girl," I say calmly. Deliberately calm just to show up the fact that she's losing it completely. "It's not my place to tell Mrs. Friesen that she can't visit her grandchildren." I harden my voice a little. "I didn't invite her." Then maybe I get a little carried away because I've glimpsed Aggie's beaten look. "If you and Mr. Friesen don't want his mother visiting perhaps you *both* should tell her. I can't do it for you."

Realizing I'm pushing my luck, I take advantage of the fact that Rhonda seems momentarily at a loss for words, hold out my hand to Aggie who rushes for it, and retreat to the kitchen to give her and Dawson a very early supper.

I don't know if Rhonda would have followed and continued the attack—I'm learning she isn't one to give up easily—but lucky for me I'm "saved by the bell." The phone rings and Rhonda spends the next half hour gossiping with one of her girlfriends.

Now I'm really dreading Saturday.

chapter six

Rosie had swallowed his story, hook, line and sinker just like he'd figured. She couldn't get over how cute the kid was. Even decided it had his ears, one round and one a bit pointy, though he couldn't see it himself. Rosie kept hugging her and saying she was the sweetest thing ever, even though the kid was still in dirty pajamas and smelled of puke. He'd tried to wash her off a bit in the motel bathroom but she started howling whenever he touched her, so he hadn't done a very good job.

Heck didn't remember much about last night. The kid had some bruises he was sure he hadn't seen before. Maybe she'd fallen out of bed or something while he was passed out.

The name business had worked out okay after all. Rosie didn't ask him, she asked the kid and then figured it out for herself.

"Leesa?" she said, looking at him. "That's a lovely name, Hector. Is it short for Elizabeth? After our mother?"

Rosie got sort of misty-eyed then. Trust her to think he'd name a kid of his after anybody around here. He hadn't even remembered Ma's real name. He'd only been three when she died. All he remembered was that everybody called her Lizzie. But he nodded. And Rosie didn't even notice that the kid looked kind of confused about the name. She was looking confused and scared anyway, so who could tell?

He hadn't stayed. He was getting nervous about getting back to Edmonton before the others decided he was ripping them off or something. Stony could be nasty when he felt like it.

By the time he left, Rosie had "Leesa" cleaned up and was handing him a package of sandwiches for the road.

"Don't you want to give your daddy a hug?" she said, shoving the kid at him.

Bad idea. The kid had started to shake and turned back, grabbing Rosie's leg.

He had to think quick. "She doesn't know me real well," he said. "And I guess she mixes me up with leaving her mother. It wasn't exactly a good scene." He decided to switch things. "But look...she's taken to you already." He was heading out the door by now, not looking back. "Stay with Aunt Rosie, Honey, she'll look after you."

He was in the truck, spitting gravel as he spun it out onto the road, before his sister could realize that he hadn't left a suitcase, toys, or any of that normal kid stuff behind.

Cora Taylor |

Oh well, he had said that the so-called girlfriend had just dumped her on him, hadn't he? Rosie could sort things out. He had other things to worry about.

If he'd only known what was going on in Edmonton, he'd have stayed in Tomahawk.

chapter seven

Leesa

Friday evening turned out pretty good after all. The phone call had been from Rhonda's friend Jackie. Jackie's real name is Jaclyn after some actress on the old *Charlie's Angels* TV show, all of which Rhonda insisted on explaining before telling me that Jackie had invited her over to the Dog Gone Saloon for a drink. She'd be back in an hour, she said. But that drink must have turned out to be quite a few because she didn't get home until after the kids and I fell asleep.

So it was a nice peaceful evening. I gave Peter his supper and he had the kids come and sit with him while he ate. I found some caramel syrup, so we all had ice cream together, and then Aggie dug out a Bugs Bunny video to watch with her dad while I gave Dawson his bath. It turned out to be the best evening since I started.

Saturday starts out just fine. Rhonda sleeps until nearly noon. Peter leaves for work early so it's quiet and I keep the kids outside all morning. I pretend we are camping on the front lawn—even make them toasted, fried-egg sandwiches so we can eat breakfast outside. Anything to keep from disturbing their mother. And they play right along—at least Aggie does—Dawson is pretty oblivious as to why we're not inside. Probably just glad to get out of his high chair. But Aggie knows. She's happy as a tick, but toward lunch time she keeps looking toward the house like she's waiting for a bomb to go off.

There's an explosion all right. If Rhonda's a pain at other times, there's nothing to match the hung-over Rhonda. We know she's up because doors slam and I can hear something breaking. No getting away from it. I have to go in and get lunch and put Dawson down for his nap.

Coward that I am, I let Dawson toddle in first.

"Keep him outta here," Rhonda screeches when we get to the kitchen.

She's down on her knees, her housecoat falling off her shoulder as she tries to pick up a broken beer bottle. She must have brought that back with her because I didn't notice any beer in the fridge before. I catch Dawson and turn Aggie around.

"Go play in your room with Dawson while I help Mummy," I say.

"Yeah," Rhonda manages to pull herself up. "Clean up this mess." She has a cigarette hanging out of her mouth and is dripping ashes all over the floor. She plops herself down at the kitchen table. "How come there's no coffee made?"

I'm scooping broken glass into the dustpan so I don't have to look at her. Peter usually makes coffee for them in the morning while I change Dawson and get him dressed, but I guess this morning he just wanted to clear out as quickly and quietly as he could.

"Do you want me to make some?"

"Do you want me to make some?" she mimicks in a snotty voice, shrill as an old alarm clock. "What do you think?" She gets up and stumbles into the living room. I can hear her mumbling curses at me but I don't care. I just hope she won't bug the kids.

By the time I have her coffee made and bring in the cup—cream no sugar, not that anything could sweeten her— she's slumped back on the couch, looking like she's asleep. Her cigarette's burned down almost to her fingers.

Tempting as it is to let her burn herself, I figure it will put her in an even worse mood so I bang the coffee down beside her and bring her the ash tray. It works. She opens her eyes, glares at me, and says, "'bout time." before butting the cigarette out and shutting her eyes again.

Good. I open a can of soup and put it on to heat, then get the kids. I carry Dawson so he doesn't face his mother. Aggie slips by her like a ghost, so we make it to the kitchen without stirring her up again.

My plan is to feed the kids and then put Dawson down for his nap while I curl up on Aggie's bed and read her stories. She doesn't usually nap but today I hope she'll fall asleep. Anything but let her stupid mother at her. What I'm going to do about supper, I don't know. All I know is that I want to steer clear of Rhonda for as long as I can.

Aggie finally falls asleep after I read both her books twice and tell her a couple of stories about a princess who looks very like her but lives in a magic castle and is looked after by a kindly old giraffe and a couple of monkeys named Roly and Poly.

It's cosy there with her cuddled against me and I only mean to close my eyes for a minute and then go out and face the Gorgon in the living room, but when I wake up it's nearly four and Dawson is howling in the next room.

By the time I get there, Rhonda is cooing over him and changing him. She's cleaned herself up and put on some makeup.

"There you are! Better get the potatoes peeled for supper." Her voice is almost civil. "I told Peter to pick up a barbeque chicken at Safeway in Edson after work. I'll drive you home as soon as he gets here."

That explains the transformation. She's talked to Peter. Now she's trying to patch things up and she doesn't want me around.

I can't believe my good luck. I won't have to stay for supper. I'll be out of this place for a whole day.

Maybe it isn't going to be too bad; I guess I can survive with Rhonda okay.

She doesn't say a word to me on the drive home, not until I open the door to get out. "By the way," she says, "my friend Jenna said her husband saw your father in Edmonton last weekend…I guess that means he's out."

I try not to show my shock as I close the door and head for the house. I know better than to turn and let her know I have no idea what she's talking about.

chapter eight

Private Journal of Clarice Warren
June 18, 2012

I hate to admit it but Ms. Madison may have been right. Not about the Guilt stuff. I was only five years old. What was I supposed to do? And anyway I didn't realize the business about the car lights and someone else being there until now. But the bit about about writing it down to get a better picture? Yes, it's definitely helped to sort out some of the "bad dream" stuff. Stuff I wouldn't have connected at the time, of course, but which makes sense now.

My sister wasn't eaten by a grizzly bear or drowned in that wild river. Mum was right, after all.

Okay. Maybe there is just a *little* guilt because I never told anybody that I'd been up with her when she went out. At first, it just got lost in the strange scariness of police and Lucky's blood. And then I guess I knew that I'd get blamed for Melissa being gone. Blamed and hated even more. Though I'm not even sure it was deliberate. How could a five-year-old be that conniving? Ms. Madison or a shrink might say it was something subconscious or crud like that, but I'm holding to the 'bad dream' theory. I was confused. And very, very scared.

Okay. So, I guess that maybe my Big Thing from that morning wasn't even about Melissa. It was about feeling totally rejected and maybe even hated by my mother. It just loomed so big that I missed the little details about that night, the car lights and all.

Of course, now that I've got all this new information, I'm not sure what I *can* do.

If I tell Madison, she'll want to tell my mother or the police. Or both. Either way I don't think there's much they can do. Not after more than twelve years. So I guess it's just going to have to be my awful secret.

Maybe I could tell Dad, but I don't see much of him now that he's remarried and got a kid. Even before that, we mostly had to meet without my mother knowing. She'd treat me like a traitor. Not that she acted as if I was up to much before, but it was just easier not to let her know. Dad arranged for me to meet Marci before he married her. We had lunch a couple of times, the three of us. And once I even met her over at SFU, where she teaches. I was prepared to hate her but she's just so nice. And I could see how happy she makes Dad. So I can't hate her. After all it wasn't *her* fault Dad left.

I've only seen my new stepsister once but she does look a lot like Melissa's baby pictures. Thank goodness my mother hasn't seen her. She'd probably flip out completely. Sometimes I think she's going to anyway.

That's why I've got to keep this new information quiet. Very, very quiet. Maybe I should even delete my journal stuff in case she snoops on my laptop. Not very likely. I could be corresponding with some porno nut for all she'd notice. My friend Shelby managed to get involved in writing to one once. Weird.

Once in a while, my mother will glance in my room. She used to yell at me about the mess. Now she doesn't. She makes a face as if both my room and I disgust her. She never comes in here now—I do my laundry, change my sheets, stuff like that. I guess I should be thankful she doesn't nose around like other mothers. But I'm not. My friends, people like Shelby, don't realize that their mothers bug them because they actually care.

Anyway, I could be building bombs in here for all she'd notice.

But that still leaves me wondering about Melissa. Maybe I'll volunteer at Child Find again for the summer. The women who volunteer there are okay. Some of them are still torn up from losing their kids, but I've never met any who are quite as out-of-it as my mother. I won't even tell her I'm doing it. Just go down and then if she happens to come in, it will be a surprise.

chapter nine

Yeah. He should have, could have, hung around Tomahawk. Rosie'd have fed him for awhile before she'd have started in on him about getting a job, supporting the kid or whatever.

It would have been a helluva lot better than going back to Edmonton.

The cops had nabbed Stony and several of the other dealers, and Stony was singing like a bird. So instead of finding a bunch of nervous junkies at Stony's, when Heck got back he'd walked into the arms of a couple of plainclothes guys.

Except he hadn't known that soon enough. He recognized one of them as a member of the Triads—turned out the guy'd been undercover then—and he figured they were there to steal his load. Like an idiot he'd carried the stuff in so he couldn't even pretend there was nothing there. So before the guy could do anything he'd gone for his knife. Just trying to protect himself and the merchandise.

The cop wasn't hurt bad but the stabbing had cooked his own goose. Not only did he get the stiffest term of any of the gang for carrying the stuff, there was an extra ten years for assaulting an officer—with intent to kill, for Pete's sake!

Guess he was lucky at that. The lab guys found the cop's blood on his knife but didn't notice that there was blood from a certain pooch that was involved in a kidnapping in B.C.

Anyway, he was locked up in Edmonton and then off in the Pen in Prince Albert so nobody'd thought to connect him with what happened by the North Thompson that night. And who'd think to look for the kid with Rosie? So he got one thing right, at least.

He managed to write to Rosie before he went in saying he was off to look for work down east so she shouldn't try to track him down. If she'd even bother to try to track him down.

chapter ten

Leesa

Out? What was Rhonda talking about?

Okay. I've heard all kinds of rumours about my dad. The big one was that he left town about seventeen years ago—he was seventeen years old at the time—because he'd got an Evansburg girl pregnant and her brothers were looking for him. And it wasn't, as was usually the case, to make him marry her either. It seemed Hector Weldon was not the kind of guy people wanted to have in their family. Whatever the threat was, it was good enough to make him head east and not come back.

I don't know how he ended up having such a bad reputation. Aunt Rosie is the best person anybody could imagine. Lots of small town guys are wild teenagers and, if they don't get killed driving too fast out on the Yellowhead, they get jobs and settle down and raise families and nobody cares. Of course, he didn't hang around.

Nobody saw him again except Aunt Rosie, the day he dropped me off.

Then people found out he was in big trouble with the law, drugs and other things, so maybe he went to jail but I figured he didn't want the responsibility of a kid and he knew I was okay here. Aunt Rosie told me he'd headed east to Ontario and would probably stay there. But now he was in Edmonton.

Suddenly the sun isn't so warm or the air so fresh. I realize I'm shivering for no reason at all. And that day off I'm looking forward to so much doesn't seem so wonderful anymore.

I make up my mind not to say anything to Aunt Rosie. Maybe Rhonda has just been pulling my chain. It's the sort of thing that would amuse her.

I walk into our kitchen and stand there. It's as if I'm waiting for it to work its magic. Ever since I was little I've connected the room with comfort somehow.

It's just a big old-fashioned farmhouse kitchen. You can still see where the old pump that used to bring water into the basin had been—there's a hole in the yellow linoleum that covers the counter. Aunt Rosie keeps a cutting board over it.

The floor creaks in a couple of places. I learned early in my life how to step over or around those spots when I sneaked downstairs for a late snack.

But the sun shines in through the yellow gingham curtains Aunt Rosie keeps clean and starched, and the old cast-iron cookstove keeps the room warm and cosy. I remember coming home from school in the winter with frozen toes and

Aunt Rosie opening the oven so I could sit in front and drink my cocoa with my feet bundled in a blanket resting on the oven door.

Warm and safe. Mainly, I guess, it's that way because Aunt Rosie is usually there.

She's there now, at the stove, with her back to me, stirring soup or something.

Everything is obviously so normal, I begin to relax.

But when she turns and I see her expression, I can tell she knows something. And it isn't good.

Of course when she sees me she puts on a brave face.

"Home already?" She bends back over the stove. When she turns again, there's a real smile on her face. "That's good!" She has a bowl of soup in her hand. "You didn't have supper, did you?"

I shake my head and sit down. I hadn't realized how hungry I was until I saw Aunt Rosie's chicken soup with the big homemade noodles floating amongst the hunks of chicken. What could be safer and more comforting than sitting here in the kitchen eating her soup?

"I'd ask you how your week went," she says as she sits down, "but I've already heard from Bessie." Her look is all sympathy. "I guess Rhonda was on the rampage. Maybe I shouldn't have got you into this. You could quit, you know."

Again, I shake my head. "The pay's good and Shauna Partridge got the job at the Village Kitchen which is about the only other place around here I could get a summer job." I slurp a few noodles. "It wasn't so bad. The kids are great and Rhonda's at work weekdays."

Aunt Rosie pours herself a cup of tea and sits down with a big sigh. "I don't know why she needs you on Saturdays, too." I bite my lip. Better not say too much. If Aunt Rosie tells Bessie it might get back to Rhonda. "If today was typical, she likes to sleep in on Saturdays," I say and leave it at that.

I'm beginning to wonder if the reason Auntie looked upset when I came in is because she heard from Bessie and is worried Rhonda is giving me a hard time. That's not too serious and for a moment I feel better. But then she sighs and stirs her tea so hard the teacup rattles on the saucer, a sure sign she's worried about something. I decide to play innocent.

"Is something wrong?"

An even bigger sigh this time.

"I'm not sure how to tell you this…" It looks like the cup is going to fly clean off the saucer. "Your father phoned today." Another sigh. "I guess I should have told you before…he's been in jail…that's why he couldn't send money for you."

I nod. "I heard rumours." I keep my voice light, matter-of-fact. I get up and ladle out another bowl of soup. Just as if we're talking about the weather or something that happened at school. "You never know what to believe in this town." I sit back down. At least I won't let the news kill my appetite. Not here in Auntie's cosy kitchen. Safe. "So, you think he'll send money now?"

I'm not about to get my hopes up. And I don't care that much. We manage the few groceries we need on the egg money and my family allowance cheque. Lucky we have that. I know Aunt Rosie had a tough time getting me on back when I first arrived. I had no birth certificate.

I must have been born at home because she hadn't been able to find any record of my birth. Hard to believe my mother hadn't bothered to register me and get the family allowance herself but who knew the story behind that part of my life? Anyway, with the help of Pastor Dobbs at Immanuel Church where I'd been going with Auntie ever since I toddled onto the scene, I had a baptismal certificate—Elizabeth Rose Weldon—so we'd finally got me a birth certificate. Auntie confessed she'd even had to guess at my birthday—May 14.

"He says he wants to come and see you." Her face is starting to crumble. "He says…"

She's almost crying now. "He says he's going to come and get you…take you to live with him."

That gets my attention. And the soup spoon freezes halfway to my mouth. And clatters back into the bowl.

"No!"

Aunt Rosie nods. She's fighting not to cry and she wins. "I told him," there's a lot of spunk in her voice now and I can imagine how it must have been on the phone, "…I told him that he had no business. No business doing that. You have a job and you have to go back to school…" She slams her fist down on the table. This time the tea cup tips over but nobody cares. "I told him he could visit but this is your home!"

I can't speak. I'm shaking again. Shivering. It's like the nightmares, except I'm wide awake.

I just sit there shaking my head. I don't even know I'm crying until I feel the tears landing on my hand. I just let them fall.

chapter eleven

Private Journal of Clarice Warren
July 7, 2012

Started working at the Child Find office this week.

No problem volunteering. Everybody's a volunteer and there are never enough of them. At least not enough people who'll come in like I did and just say, "Can I help? What would you like me to do?" At first Mrs. Hansen, who runs the office, just had me sorting pamphlets and unpacking some office supplies, but when she found out I knew my way around a computer pretty well, she just gave me this big, happy smile and handed me some stuff to input.

So I spent the morning going through files. All the lost Canadian children, and even a few from the US. I hadn't realized that "Child" seems to mean anybody who disappeared before they were thirty. There was even somebody who'd disappeared at the age of thirty-two or something—my math isn't that hot and I got tired of trying to subtract birth years from when they went missing to figure out ages. Anyway, I was mostly interested in those who'd gone missing when they were two or three years old, like Melissa had.

She was there, of course, with her picture from around the time she'd disappeared and the one representing what she'd look like now—the fancy portrait in the living room. I recognize her two-year-old picture, too. It was from one Dad had taken of the two of us, sitting side by side on the picnic table when we were on that camping trip. In the original photo, I've got a piece of toast in my hand that Dad had helped me toast on the little camp stove. Except in this one, there's just Melissa, and I was cut out. Of course.

I know. I need to get a grip. Why would they leave you in the picture? Nobody's looking for you. And I have to try to stop feeling that "out-of-it, nobody-wants-to-find-you" resentment stuff. But it's hard. I've been feeling hurt and then mad about everything all these years, I guess.

Anyhow, I came up with a suggestion that made Mrs. H's day: cross-referencing the missing kids by their ages when they disappeared, how long they've been missing, locations, gender, whether they had siblings who disappeared too, and stuff like that. At first I was worried that she'd think it was a dumb idea, but as I told her all about it, she stared at me as if I'd just invented the wheel or discovered the cure for Cancer or something. I guess she's not too familiar with the miracle of Excel spreadsheets.

So, I've got a summer job whenever I want it. Volunteer, so no pay, of course, although Mrs. Hansen says she's going to try and get something through the Hire-A-Student program now that I've got a project.

Volunteering means I don't have to go every day but I have so far. Even keeping office hours like Mrs. H. She's always so happy to see me show up, looking up when I walk in, a little surprised, like she didn't expect me. She's started bringing in snacks for me. Things she bakes herself—Naniamo bars and apple crisp.

I have to admit that I'm enjoying being with Mrs. H. She's cheerful and thoughtful, so the office, even with all those lost-kid posters around, is a nice place to be. Okay, I'll admit it, I like Mrs. H. and I think she likes me, too. Hard to believe. I keep looking at her just to be sure, but when she smiles at me, there's a nice look in her eyes.

What I'm doing is interesting, too. I'm actually starting to enjoy myself—whenever I'm able to get by those cute little faces and stop wondering what happened to them, of course.

chapter twelve

Leesa

"There...there, my pet."

Aunt Rosie's voice. Always the same, always there for me. I can't imagine life without it. Except I suddenly realize that it isn't the same. Before, those words had always come with a calm voice. A sad voice, maybe, but comforting. Now it is more than sad. There are tears in her voice. It shakes me. Makes me look up and that hurts more than anything. No matter how many problems we've had, in all the time I've known her I've never seen my aunt break down.

There is a fist in my chest—but this makes it shake.

And then I'm angry.

"No!" I say. "I won't go! He can't make me!" Obviously the Spunk is with me because the madder I get, the surer I am that I can't be forced to go. "He has no right! And besides he's got a criminal record. No judge would award him custody. Pastor Dobbs can testify to how well you've cared for me."

Aunt Rosie doesn't say anything. Just sits there looking desolate.

She doesn't have to say anything. I can read the hopelessness. I know that to challenge my father, we'd have to go to court, and that would cost money—big money. Way more than we could ever raise.

"Legal Aid!" I say. The idea strikes me like a lightning stroke or like the little light bulb cartoonists put over people's head when they want to indicate a bright idea. One of the girls at school had a sister who used Legal Aid to get divorced from an abusive husband. "It's for people who can't afford lawyers…and that's definitely us!" I'm looking at Aunt Rosie, wanting her to hear the hope in my voice and know that there is a chance.

Whether she hears the hope or just feels it, Aunt Rosie perks up.

"You're right! I'll talk to Pastor Dobbs after church tomorrow, too, and get his advice. We can fight this." She straightens her shoulders and gives me a hug before she turns back to the stove.

I am an expert reader of hugs. Aunt Rosie's anyway. There are the "there, there, my pet" consoling ones and there are the "you're fine, don't make a fuss" ones which really mean "just get on with it and quit feeling sorry for yourself." The one she gave me before was unique. Then she was so despairing that it felt as if there was no consolation for either of us in the hug, just two people clinging together without hope. The hug she gave me just now seemed to fit into the third category, except I'm not sure. She's looking into the soup pot so I can't see her face. Then she begins to fill a bowl for herself and I know I'm right. We're going to be all right.

One thing I knew for sure: Aunt Rosie won't give me up easily. The kitchen starts to seem like a happy place once more. My soup is cold but it's still delicious, and now I can swallow again.

"When your father phones again, I won't let him bully me."

I smile, encouraging her. "Spunk," I say. I realize that I can handle my own bad dreams and worries, but Aunt Rosie's are another matter.

She doesn't seem to hear me. She just sits, sipping her soup and staring past me. "He used to bully me all the time when we were kids. I was much older but once he was big enough, he'd twist my arm behind my back all the time." She stops eating and just stares at the wall beyond. "Sometimes, he'd do it to get me to do something or give him something he wanted. But sometimes…" She shakes her head as if she can't understand. "I think he did it just…for fun."

Now I wish she'd stop. I don't want to know this. How could anybody hurt someone as kind as Aunt Rosie? What kind of person? Besides, I know that she pretty well raised my father from the age of three when their mother, my Grandma Lizzie, died.

I'm wracking my brain for some way to change the subject. During school I'd have pleaded homework and escaped.

"Do you want me to do the chores?"

Chores at night in the summer just consist of gathering eggs and closing the henhouse door once the chickens have gone to roost.

Aunt Rosie seems glad of the distraction. "Good idea. I think there's been a skunk coming around, so watch for it." She's up now, taking our dishes to the sink. "I think I'll get Papa's gun down and check it out in case I have to shoot the thing."

I step out into the Alberta evening. The sun is still high even though it's after seven o'clock, so I have to chase the last few hens inside for the night. I grab the egg basket and start picking the eggs out of the nests. One hen is still on the nest and she pecks at me when I try to reach under her, but I push her head back and get the eggs anyway. When I was little, I'd just skip the nests the hens were on, and sometimes Aunt Rosie would find nearly a dozen eggs next time she came. Not good to leave them. You can't sell "Fresh Eggs" if they've been left for a day or two. I make sure that there's nothing hiding behind the feed pails by the door or under any of the rows of nesting boxes, just in case Auntie's skunk is inside before I close the door. Bonnie, our big old collie is waiting for me, wagging her tail.

"Did you miss me, girl? You'd bark if there was a skunk in there, you wouldn't let me get skunked, would you?" Probably not. Her senses aren't what they used to be these days, poor thing. But we love her.

Auntie is checking the old rifle out when I came back in the kitchen. We are both pretty good with that gun. I've been shooting magpies with it since I was a kid. When I was ten I declared war on magpies. I'd had a lovely little bantie hen who'd hatched out thirteen little fluffball chicks. Maybe thirteen was an unlucky number. If the hen fluffed out her feathers and spread her wings, she could just barely manage to cover the whole clutch. When I left for school that morning, I'd seen a magpie bothering her but the bus was coming and I had to run.

When I got off the school bus that afternoon the first thing I did was go to check my chicks. There was only one left. And there were two magpies now, one in front of and one behind the poor mother hen. Before I could get the gate open and go in the pen to help, the magpie in the back had grabbed the chick and bitten into it with its cruel beak.

That was when I learned to use the old rifle. I lined up cans until I was a good shot, and then I went after the magpies.

It took awhile. I lay on my stomach behind the lilac bush with the dish full of dog food out in front of the house until the magpies came. The first one was easy but it took awhile after I'd shot it for the second one to come back. Aunt Rosie worried because I got pretty badly mosquito-bitten, lying out there, but I finally got the second magpie. Maybe they weren't the two who'd killed my chicks but I like to believe they were.

"No skunk tonight," I say, putting the basket by the sink and wiping the eggs one by one before putting them in cartons to go in the fridge.

Aunt Rosie doesn't look up. "Not tonight," she says.

chapter thirteen

Rosie had her nerve, telling him he couldn't take the kid. He'd like to see the look on her face if he told her the truth— that she wasn't even related. That the girl she thought was Elizabeth Weldon was somebody else altogether.

Yeah, he'd like to do that but if he did then he'd be caught for kidnapping. Rosie'd probably think she had to report it, even if it meant she really would have to lose the kid.

Not that she'd ever see her again when he took her this time. He had plans for the girl. Probably had a body by now. She'd had the same kind of fluffy blond hair her big sister had, so she'd probably turned out to be a bit of a looker.

And he had a few connections he'd picked up in prison. His original plan had been to leave her until she was five or six and then get her. He liked them that age. No fighting. Not like some of the older ones you had to bash around when they fought back. Some of them could kick a guy where it hurt, though they wouldn't do it again if he had anything to do with it.

But that was before he got that extra sentence. So she wouldn't be a cute little kid, but he could still use her. He'd made some connections. Maybe bring her back to Edmonton or even farther east, and introduce her to enough crack or meth to get her hooked, then move her on to something stronger so she wouldn't object when he put her to work.

Turk, his "roommate" in the Pen said he'd help him get set up. Turk only had a little while to go before he was on the street again.

And he said he had connections in L.A. Big time.

Meanwhile he'd make a few trips to Tomahawk and play Nice Daddy. Make Rosie feel sorry for him because he missed "his baby girl" all these years. If Rosie went along with a few visits, he'd suggest taking the kid into Edmonton, show her the mall, and take her to a movie. Promise to have her back the same day, if necessary.

Rosie should know he never kept his promises but by then it would be too late.

He and the girl could disappear. Eventually cross the border. Turk would know a guy who could fix them up with passports.

It made him chuckle. How many kids got kidnapped twice, he wondered.

chapter fourteen

Leesa

Aggie looks so happy to see me, it almost makes going back Sunday night tolerable. I am still finishing supper when Peter arrives. Rhonda makes sure he picks me up early enough that I'll be in time to give the kids their baths and put them to bed. She's following Aunt Rosie's "24-hour day-off" stipulation to the letter.

You'd have thought the way Aggie hugs me goodnight that I've been gone a month. A little Rhonda goes a long way.

It's easy to fall into the routine now and the days with the kids are kind of fun. I've brought a bunch of old magazines from home, so Aggie and I are getting back into the scrapbooking thing. Peter has even slipped us a few snapshots of the kids so we're able to put their faces in some of the scenes. Cute stuff, like Dawson's face on a cowboy riding the range, or Aggie in a spiffy, red sports car or pasted over the head of a movie star in a designer gown at the Oscars.

I didn't have any trouble persuading her that it's our secret. She knows better than to let her mother spoil something special.

Wednesday night, while I was doing the dishes and getting my usual lecture from Rhonda, Aggie even showed her dad the scrapbook.

"He likes it!" She beamed at me when I tucked her into bed. Then solemnly, "And I made him promise not to tell!"

Now, while Dawson has his afternoon naps, we tell each other stories about Princess Aggie and Cowboy Dawson.

I'm glad the days are going quickly though. I try to phone Aunt Rosie every other day when I get a minute. The talk with Pastor Dobbs has helped. He's going to help us get connected with someone from Legal Aid when the time comes.

And we guess it will come, although my dad hasn't called again. It's kind of nerve-wracking wondering whether he'll call or just show up, and Aunt Rosie says she feels as if she's "waiting for a bomb to go off."

I can sympathize. Living with Rhonda is sort of like that. When she's around I feel as if I'm tiptoeing through a minefield. Especially on Saturday mornings.

She was out late Friday night again. Which meant that we had a lovely time Friday evening. After Dawson was in bed, Aggie brought out her scrapbook and began to tell her dad some of the stories we'd been making up. I wish Bessie could have been there. She'd have loved to see her son and granddaughter cuddled up, laughing over the pictures and trying to top each other's silly stories.

It was actually a bit embarrassing, the way Peter kept

thanking me afterward. It made me scurry off to bed a little earlier than I might have.

Today, we're having another Saturday picnic breakfast on the lawn. This time we pretend we are camping. Even make a tent out of a blanket. Funny though, I guess I'm not much of a camper. I feel strange pretending to sleep in the tent with the kids. I'm almost relieved when we hear Rhonda crashing around inside.

"Do you think there's a bear in the house?" Aggie says to Dawson. She's grinning, happy to keep up the make-believe.

I'd love to play along but I'm afraid to—Rhonda wouldn't like the bear part—and I don't want to get Aggie in trouble.

"Mummy bear!" whooped Dawson, who obviously doesn't know about hangovers yet.

He's up and heading for the house at a fast toddle, while Aggie and I break camp as fast as we can.

Mostly it's a repeat of the previous Saturday without the breakage. I make sure I don't fall asleep, though. When I go downstairs, Rhonda's waiting with the latest Dog Gone Saloon gossip.

"So has your dad been out to see you yet? Or maybe you're moving to Edmonton to live with him in the fall?"

I'm sorry Aggie's followed me downstairs because she looks so crestfallen at that idea. And I don't want Rhonda to pick up on that look; I know that even mothers who don't like their kids get jealous if the kid likes someone else.

"Nope," I say cheerily, for Aggie's sake. "That's a rumour even the National Enquirer wouldn't accept." I turn and smile at Aggie, "I'm staying right here!"

I can tell Rhonda isn't too thrilled at my response. I figure she's been hoping for some insider information to pass along the Dog Gone Saloon grapevine. I'm rewarded for my lack of co-operation by getting to scrub both bathrooms before I get to leave that night. But then Peter drives me home, so I don't have to put up with her any longer.

This time I don't even get to go into the house before my "happy-to-be-home" bubble bursts.

There's a strange car in the yard—a black, late-model Lexus with Alberta plates—but I'm sure it doesn't belong to anybody from around Tomahawk. I don't want to get out of the car, and I sit there so long that Peter Friesen is gives me a funny look.

"Is everything all right, Leesa?"

I force myself to open the door but can't get out yet. "Could you…would you…mind waiting a minute?" I stammer, wishing I could think of some way to invite him in. "Please? Just until I see if everything's okay?"

I guess he's heard the rumours, too. Maybe Rhonda's given him the latest news from the Dog Gone Saloon. It's probably all over town. Anyway, he's obviously figured out what's going on because he's thinking more clearly than I am.

"Leave your backpack," he says firmly. "I'll drive away as if I'm leaving…" He pauses and looks grim. "I'll go about a mile and then come back as if I just noticed you've forgotten it. When I drive back in the yard and you come out, I'll know everything's okay. If not, I'll come in."

He looks at me right in the eye then. "Okay?"

I don't know how he knows how scared I am, but I could

have hugged him. I'm so grateful somebody has a grip on things and knows what to do.

My feet are moving toward the house now, although I wish I could just stop and stay there. By the time I get to the door, Peter has backed the car around. The lights flash across the house and then the car disappears down the lane and out onto the road. I just let my feet carry me on inside.

Aunt Rosie is sitting at the kitchen table, the usual cup of tea and teapot there. She's facing me as I come in so all I can see is the back of the man's head. Greasy blond hair that hangs down over the collar of a black leather jacket. I can see he's wearing jeans and boots, heavy ones, not work boots but probably steel-toed.

Then he stands up and turns around and I am face-to-face with my father.

chapter fifteen

Private Journal of Clarice Warren
August 1, 2012

Been working at Child Find for a month now and yesterday afternoon was the first time my mother showed up at the office. The look on her face when she saw me was priceless. Did she think I'd been out hanging around the malls every day all summer? But she never asked where I went and I never told.

Even better than that first look of shock was the expression that came over her face when Mrs. Hanson started singing my praises. Total disbelief! I almost laughed out loud.

I just keep reliving it, feeling the warm fuzzies.

"I don't know what I'd do without Clarice!" Mrs. H. kept rambling on as she poured tea and put out the Nanaimo bars. "She's such a joy to have around…so helpful and co-operative."

She was standing behind my mother's chair so she couldn't see her face. But she patted Mum on the shoulder and said sympathetically, "Your daughter must be a great comfort to you!"

That was when I choked, got the tea up in my nose, and had to run for the can, so I didn't see my mother's response. If she'd had a mouthful of tea she'd probably have choked, too.

Anyway, when I came back out they were talking about an upcoming meeting. Mrs. H. had cleaned up my mess so I just got back to work.

These days, I'm tracking down newpaper write-ups about a kid in Florida who disappeared while being babysat by her father's seventeen-year-old girlfriend. Apparently the girlfriend is a crack addict and doesn't know how or when the kid was taken. The dad doesn't sound much better but he's been given custody, since the mother is a drunk. Makes you wonder what kind of life that little girl can look forward to. A far cry from our Melissa, with parents who adored her, even if her big sister had a serious case of sibling rivalry.

It got me thinking. Would Melissa and I have become friends once she was older and we could play together? What would life have been like with a teenaged sister and a mother who wasn't tied in knots all the time? Maybe Dad wouldn't have felt he had to leave and we'd still be a family.

While Mrs. Hansen talked to my mom, I got kind of lost in that file—working at Child Find does that to me—so Mrs. H. actually had to come over and tap me on the shoulder to get my attention.

She said that it was the end of the day and that I could get a ride back with my mom.

I looked over at Mum, surprised that she'd offered to take me but I could tell by her face that it was Mrs. H.'s idea, not hers. I almost said no, but then I figured Mrs. Hansen would wonder why and maybe worry that something was wrong. So I shut down the computer, got my stuff, and followed my mother out.

Well, that was a fun ride home. If I'd been nourishing the idea my mother would be pleased or even willing to talk about the office in a friendly way, I should've known better.

NEWS FLASH

So I'm eating take-out up in my room when the phone rings. I've had my iPhone turned off all day so when I checked a little while ago, there were about a dozen text messages from my friend Shelby. Trouble. Big time. But since she's a major Drama Queen, I wasn't too excited. I figured I'll have something to eat and then phone her and get the whole story. But then the phone rings so I figure what the hell.

She barely gives me a chance to say, "Hey," and she's off.

"You know that guy I've been writing to online? I found out he's IN JAIL!".

"Probably a good thing," I interrupted. The only way to talk to Shelby is to interrupt her. "I mean he can't do much harm from there, can he?" I took another leisurely bite of chicken.

"No…no…NO! You don't understand! He's getting out soon—he says he's coming to Vancouver!"

"So what? You weren't dumb enough to tell him where you live were you?

Except, yeah. She IS dumb enough. And I'm heading over to her place now so she can freak out at me in person.

chapter sixteen

Leesa

What did I expect, seeing my father face-to-face? He's a stranger. I don't remember him at all.

I've wondered what he looked like. Aunt Rosie didn't seem to have any pictures of him except when he was a little kid. So I would wonder: Did I look like him or my mother? Curiosity. That's all. That's what I expected to feel.

And for a moment that's all there is.

He isn't much taller than me, this stranger. Then I'm memorizing his face. He has close-set green eyes, the same colour as Aunt Rosie's except hers are kind. At first glance, I can't see any sign of softness in his, even though he's looking at a daughter he's supposed to love. He has one of those little under-the-bottom-lip, wispy goatees that hockey players seem to favour. It doesn't do anything for him. I feel a surge of relief that I don't look a bit like him. I wonder if he has a picture of my mother so I can see what she looked like.

Not that I care to find her—if she didn't want me, why should I want her? Anyway, Aunt Rosie is all the mother I need.

For a minute, we just stand there looking. Sizing each other up. Nobody moves except Aunt Rosie, who puts her teacup down and stands up to come around to us.

Then he moves toward me.

It doesn't happen then. It happens moments later, when he begins to speak.

His voice isn't loud. It's cold and thin. Quiet. But it brings a chill to the room. I begin to shiver. Aunt Rosie used to say "someone's walking on my grave" whenever she had misgivings about something. That's what I feel. Irrational fear.

I don't even know what he's saying. My name, perhaps? I miss everything else. Because that's when I start to shake. Not trembling. Shaking. Like convulsions. I try to back away but I can't. It's as if my feet are nailed to the floor. And he keeps looking me up and down and moving toward me.

"Hector—" Aunt Rosie says his name and he stops moving.

But he keeps talking. The sound of his voice goes on and on. I don't recognize words at all, just the tone of it stabbing, jabbing into me. And I am still shaking.

But I can move now because Aunt Rosie is there beside me, her arm around me pulling me around the table. Away from him.

"There, there, pet!" She sits me down in the chair where she'd been sitting on the other side of the table. The yellow, gingham seat cushion is still warm. Aunt Rosie-warm. She pours me a cup of tea but my hands are holding onto the chair and the cushion and I can't move them to pick up the cup. I know I'll spill the tea if I do. I'm holding the chair with a death grip as if it is the only solid thing and if I let go the convulsions will be so severe that I'll fall right off onto the worn linoleum floor.

Aunt Rosie pulls a chair close to me and sits down. I know she won't leave me. I hope she won't leave me.

My father comes back to the table and sits down right across from me. Too bad. He's drinking tea but I can see him staring at me over the top of the cup. Hard eyes. At least he isn't talking. Not hearing his voice helps.

"Did you have a good day? I hope Rhonda wasn't too hard on you…" Aunt Rosie's voice is soothing, concerned, and I'm grateful she's filling the awkward silence so my father won't be tempted to speak again. I just wish she wouldn't ask me questions as if she expects me to be able to speak.

"Okay," I manage. Not a whisper, more of a croak.

"I told you Leesa had a summer job, didn't I?"

Don't ask him questions, I want to shriek. Don't let him speak.

He doesn't. All I can hear is the ticking of the old Baby Ben clock Aunt Rosie keeps on the shelf above the dish-towel hanger.

And then, God bless him, Peter Friesen's car is driving into the yard. He is going to have to come in. There's no way I can get up and go outside.

Aunt Rosie gets up and goes to the window. "That's Peter Friesen. I wonder why?"

"Pete Friesen?" The voice again. A different tone this time. Edgy. Nervous. "What's he doing here?"

I am still hanging onto my chair for dear life but I can make out words now. And I can think again. My father doesn't know what Pete's connection is. So Aunt Rosie told him that I had a summer job but not where. Not like her not to be open about something like that. Is she afraid he'll bother me at work? Maybe I'm not the only one who fears him? After all, fear is the reason I'm reacting the way I am. Fear like the nightmares, though I don't know why.

Then Peter knocks on the door and Auntie's there inviting him in. She insists he join us for tea, once he's brought in the backpack and been thanked.

At first, neither my father nor I move as Peter comes to sit down, but then my father jumps up and grabs Peter's hand and starts pumping it like they're old buddies.

"Petey! Haven't seen you since high school. How you been?"

"Heck." Peter nods. His voice is guarded, not unfriendly. There's not much warmth in his smile, though. "Can't complain...you?"

"Doin' okay...movin' around..."

Again the voice is different. Hearty in a phony sort of way. That voice isn't scary. I'm beginning to relax. Especially with Peter sitting at the table drinking tea and having a piece of Aunt Rosie's coffee cake. I even manage to pick up the teacup and get it to my lips without spilling, though I only pretend to drink. I'm not sure if I can swallow anything. My throat is just a hard lump.

I listen, sort of listen, while my father quizzes Peter about various people they'd been at school with and where they were, though it's obvious even to me that he could care less. I notice Peter is diplomatic enough not to ask my father where he's been and what he's been up to.

My aunt keeps pouring more tea and I keep pretending to drink it until she notices that my cup is still full and dumps it to give me a fresh cup.

I'm just trying to get rid of the lump in my throat when I yawn.

"Poor Leesa," Aunt Rosie is all over me, "you must be exhausted."

She picks up my father's empty cake plate. "And you've got a long drive back to Edmonton…you'd better get started!"

I don't know if my father expected to stay overnight but he can't very well protest in front of Peter. So they both stand up and start walking to the door.

I finally manage to speak. "Thank you for bringing my backpack, Mr. Friesen," I choke out. "I'm very grateful."

He just nods as he goes out behind my father but I'm pretty sure he understands what I mean.

Aunt Rosie stands at the window until both cars are out on the main road. Then she goes to the cupboard drawer and takes out a couple of table knives. We don't usually lock our doors—don't even have a key for the old-fashioned lock on the front door. But she slides the flat knife blade along the doorjamb so that the handle is firm against the door and nobody can open the door from outside. She does the same thing with the door to the back porch.

"You know," she says, "I think I'll get Wilf Owen at the hardware store to put in a couple of those doorknobs you can lock." She's mumbling as she follows me up the stairs. "Should have done it long ago…"

I don't say anything, just hug her hard before I go into my room.

chapter seventeen

Private Journal of Clarice Warren
August 2, 2012

No work today, long weekend. I'm going to really miss seeing Mrs. H. Busy day on Saturday. I stayed over at Shelby's after her Friday night freak-out. Really didn't want to but I couldn't just leave her hanging. Getting up early to go to work every morning is a bit of a drag and I had been looking forward to the Saturday morning sleep-in. But whatever. I could have told Shelby no, but she's about the closest thing to a friend I have—one more chick who's always in trouble at school, which is why we hang together.

We started out sitting on her bed, drinking beer she smuggled up from the basement where her dad keeps it. Pretty crappy stuff—one of those light beers. Her dad isn't dumb. He keeps the hard stuff locked up, so I guess he doesn't care about the beer or maybe he thinks Shelby wouldn't be bothered. He should know her better than that.

Anyway, her parents had gone over to Victoria on the

ferry to visit some friends and wouldn't be back until Sunday night which is why she panicked. Normally she really digs being alone but like I said, she thinks this guy may be out of jail now. Maybe even in Vancouver looking for her.

I didn't bother to mention that I probably wasn't going to be much protection for her—didn't have the heart to tell her. She finally managed to calm down. Just sat cross-legged on the bed chewing on her black fingernails.

The black polish is a hangover from her weeks being Goth. I'm not sure why she gave it up. She says the Goth kids at school were too weird for her. I find that hard to believe. More likely she was too weird for them but I shut up about it. Shelby finds herself a new persona every few weeks. The funniest was her jock phase. Shelby, the couch potato, actually joined the track team. Strangely enough, that lasted longer than any of her other attempts to "belong." Probably because she found the 'body boys' turned her on.

Unlike Shelby, I do not bother with the cliques. It's easier to keep to yourself.

Once she calmed down enough to talk, I asked her if she'd ever texted any messages to this guy on her cell phone.

She looked surprised. "No, just chatting online."

I said, "Good, so at least he doesn't have your phone number! You might have had trouble convincing your dad to change phone numbers." Sometimes Shelby can be sooo clueless.

She had already ordered pizza before I got there, and we kidded around with the delivery guy for awhile. I was starving by the time he left since I hardly had any of the KFC my mother bought earlier.

So I waited for Shelby to get around to telling me why she was so scared while we destroyed the pizza. When we'd talked on the phone, she couldn't wait for me to get over, like she couldn't stand being alone another minute.

But once she got me over there, she was annoyingly casual. Waiting for me to take the lead. Almost like whole thing was supposed to have been my idea.

I started licking cheese strings off my fingers and pretending I'm not really interested in what she's been up to. I've learned that's the best way to get Shelby to tell you stuff. Finally, I asked, "Well? What exactly have you been writing to this creep?"

She sat there forever, guzzling her beer and taking her sweet time about answering. I felt like giving her the finger and heading home. But when she finally started to talk, I changed my mind, and a good thing I did, too. At first she tried to explain what sort of stuff she and the creepo had talked about, but I could tell that she was just paraphrasing, skimming over the stuff she's written to the guy. I let her babble on for a while but what with the beer and pizza combo, I just wanted to get it over with and crash for the night.

Finally she turned on the computer and showed me some of their chat sessions. And then I was wide awake.

chapter eighteen

This is going to take longer than he thought. At least if "Daddy's" first visit is anything to go by.

But the kid's a looker all right. Even better than he'd expected.

She has a kind of fresh, unspoiled, country-girl beauty. Very saleable. Too bad she wouldn't keep that once he got her on the drugs. But even without it he could see she had a great bod. Talk about J. Lo booty. He figured she was worth a bit of extra work. And time.

How he got off on the wrong foot with "his daughter," he isn't sure. No way she could possibly remember him. Maybe she picked up some vibes from Rosie. Rosie, trying to be nice to her kid brother, but looking like a deer in the headlights when he first arrived. Took him a while to calm her down. He managed to convince her that he wasn't going to go for custody—that he'd changed his mind about that. Made her think her arguments about keeping the girl here in Tomahawk to finish school made sense. He gave Rosie a bunch of bull about him realizing that she could give Leesa a better home than he could. Of course, Rosie fell for it.

"Maybe," he was doing the humble bit, "maybe I can just come and visit her here?" Didn't even mention that he'd like to take her to Edmonton once in a while. That could come later.

He was glad the girl wasn't there so he could clear the way with Rosie. Get her to relax a bit. He thought he was doing good, too. She was coming along nicely. Funny though. She told him Leesa had a summer job and then wouldn't tell him where. Never mind. He'd figured if he played it cool, she'd loosen up.

"Working at the cafe? The Village Kitchen?" Real casual, like he didn't care. She's too young to get hired at the Dog Gone Saloon.

"No. Babysitting." That's it. Rosie just clammed up.

He tried again. "That's great! Anybody I know?"

"No," said The Clam. So he dropped it. He figured he'd suss it out soon enough. No problem.

Then the kid showed up. He'd already decided maybe he'd better go slow, no hugs or anything, but when he tried talking to her she went all funny. Shaking and just staring past him. He almost said something like, "Is that any way to greet your Daddy?" joking-like, but thought better of it. Her reaction was too rough.

At least she didn't run. Kinda looked like she would if

she could, but she seemed sort of paralyzed. Except for the shaking. So he finally shut up and let Rosie handle things while they sat around drinking tea out of them stupid teacups.

Then who the hell shows up but that jerk, Pete Friesen.

Turns out she'd left her backpack in his car when he drove her home, so it's obvious who she's babysitting for. He'd heard Pete married some skank from Hinton and had a couple of brats. So phooey to Rosie trying to make a big mystery of things.

He'd been hoping to just hang out there late enough that Rosie would let him bunk over. And he would've just stayed put on the couch or whatever, too. No point in screwing things up at this point. But Rosie shooed Pete and him out 'cause she said the girl is too tired and he's got "a long drive back to Edmonton." As if he hasn't driven all night before, a lot farther than that.

But he went, like a good boy. And followed Pete just to make sure of where he's living. Maybe when Leesa has softened up a bit he'll drop by and visit her at work. See what Pete's kids look like. Why not?

There's time. And the girl's definitely worth the wait.

chapter nineteen

Leesa

By Sunday night, things are almost back to normal. After church, Aunt Rosie and I go to Bessie's for soup and a sandwich, and except for a great feeling of relief when we turn in our lane and I don't see a strange car parked there, there's nothing unusual about the day.

Bessie offers to drive me over to her son's, so that helps me relax, too. I don't have to worry that Rhonda'll be picking me up. Every little bit of time away from Ms. Misery, as Bessie calls her daughter-in-law, is a gift, as far as I am concerned.

"You know," Bessie says cheerfully as we park in front of the Friesen house, "I think I'll just volunteer to deliver you every Sunday night! Gives me a chance to see the kids."

Yep, I think, and Peter's there so Rhonda can't throw a hissy-fit.

"That would be nice," I say. But I'm afraid I'll pay for being that much more connected with Bessie in Rhonda's eyes. It's not a big worry though. I figure that Rhonda'll put a stop to Bessie's visits one way or another.

The good thing is that Aggie's big, happy greeting for me has to be spread to her grandmother, which means that Rhonda can't blame me for stealing her daughter's affection. Not that she's ever acted as if Aggie means more than dirt to her before. It's the principle, and I'm beginning to think Rhonda's mean enough for just about anything.

For example, she's saved the supper clean-up for me on top of putting the kids to bed, but they're clamouring for some time with Bessie, so Peter suggests that he and his mother do the bedtime stuff. That should have been a Good Thing for me but it frees Rhonda up, so she hangs around the kitchen while I clean up and load the dishwasher.

"I hear your dad was visiting you," she says, blowing smoke as she leans against the counter. She's watching me like a hawk, either because she wants to see my reaction or in case I miss a spot when I scour the sink. "That must've been nice."

I wonder how much Peter has told her. Not much, I suppose, but he'd have had to explain why it took him so long to get back after driving me home.

I take my time answering. Acting busy. Shaking Comet onto the cloth and making like the sink is even greasier than it is. Finally, I just shrug.

"Of course, you haven't seen him since you were little, have you?" She's staring at me and I can see she isn't going to let me off the hook.

I figure she knows the whole story—about the mother who

Cora Taylor | **83**

dumped me on my dad, who then dumped me on Aunt Rosie. Even though she hadn't married Pete until after I started school, she'd have heard it from him or Bessie or just about anybody in town. And now it will be hot news again. I can imagine that rumours are flying at the Dog Gone Saloon these days.

"How's he looking?" she persists.

I'm wiping the pots and pans and stowing them under the cupboard by the sink, wishing she'd go away.

"Well," I say finally, "I don't have much to compare it with since I don't remember him from before."

I plop a clean ashtray down on the counter beside her and go to the broom closet and get the dust mop. Make a point of mopping up the ashes that had fallen from her cigarette.

I keep hoping that Peter and Bessie will come back downstairs but no luck. They've tucked Dawson in bed but are still in Aggie's room. And much as I want a break from Rhonda, I can't begrudge Aggie the pleasure of having her bedtime stories.

Rhonda isn't finished. "Jackie says Heck Larkin was quite the rebel when they were in junior high…before he got himself expelled for punching the gym teacher!"

That catches me by surprise and I guess it shows. Rhonda looks pleased that she's finally got a reaction from me. I don't say anything. Still, she can tell I'm interested so she does the long pause, takes a couple of slow drags on her cigarette, and peers at me through the smoke like the cat that ate the canary.

"I guess it didn't help his case that the gym teacher was female and weighed about 98 pounds soaking wet." Another dramatic pause. Rhonda staring thoughtfully at her cigarette.

I wonder what's coming next and quickly put the mop away so I can get out of the room. I have my back turned when she comes up with her next line.

"Still, Jackie figured that Mrs. Wendell could have cleaned his clock if she hadn't been pregnant!"

I can hear Peter and Bessie coming down the stairs now so I don't look back, but Rhonda had the last word anyway.

"Hey!" she calls after me. "You forgot to set the table for breakfast!"

*   *   *

The rest of the week doesn't go too badly. Aggie and I finish one scrapbook and start another. I'd like to get her going on some other crafts, but I know anything we do has to be hidden from Rhonda and we don't have that much space. We're keeping the scrapbooks under Aggie's mattress since I'm the one who changes the beds all the time now. I worry about what will happen when school starts again and I'm not babysitting anymore.

At least Aggie's going to be in kindergarten half days in September, so she'll have some time away from Rhonda.

"My mother," Aggie informs me one day, "is going to work part-time nights when you can't come any more." She has her worried look back, the one I've tried to dispel. I know she's ill-at-ease about having Rhonda around all day.

"But you'll be at school!" I say and it cheers her up. I don't bother to mention that she'll only be going half days at first.

Friday afternoon when I bring Dawson down from his nap, Aggie is standing in the living room looking out of the picture window.

"There's that man in the black car again," she says. "I wonder why he doesn't come in?"

I get there just in time to see it pull away, but I recognize the Lexus all right.

Aggie can't remember how many times she's noticed it and I don't want to press her and make her wonder about it. Obviously though, it's been parked out front more than once this week.

"Sometimes…" she says, "the man doesn't stop…just drives by." She's sensing my concern and trying to reassure me. "But he goes real slow, so he won't run over any children or anything…"

"Oh, that's good!" I say trying to sound as though everything is fine. But as far as I'm concerned it isn't.

I'm actually glad to see Rhonda when she comes home from work that day.

chapter twenty

Private Journal of Clarice Warren
August 3, 2012

You read about online predators. People who pretend they're somebody they're not. And why wouldn't some lonely girl send a guy a picture of someone prettier than she is? It's kind of like a role-playing game. And everybody has heard about the fourteen-year-old boy who claimed he was a curvy blond chick just to lure some old guy into a hot correspondence. Just a cool joke.

But then you find out sometimes it's not a joke when you read about a porno type luring a young girl away from her home and getting her in trouble—or worse. The irony is that most parents can't do anything about it because their kids' computer skills are a hundred times better than theirs.

Shelby's parents are definitely typical that way, though I know that they try from time to time to check up on her. She thinks it's a huge joke.

But sitting at her computer, she was not amused. And

neither was I when I saw the stuff the guy has been writing to her. Of course, in order to show me that stuff, she also had to show me what she's written to him. I tried to just read and not comment but finally it got to me.

"Were you out of your screwed-up mind?" I burst out.

Normally Shelby'd have been all defensive but if I needed any reminder that she was scared shitless her reaction proved it. She just kept wailing miserably about how totally dumb she is.

Which is amazing—for Shelby to admit she'd made a mistake, I mean.

I didn't have the heart to give her the gears anymore, so I stopped pointing out all the dumb stuff she'd written and started picking out details that might be important. Clues.

"At least I didn't tell him where I live or give him my phone number or anything stupid like that!" she said.

Duh.

But here's a list of what he DOES know:

1. Her first name.
2. What she looks like (she sent him a PICTURE!!!)
3. Her favourite place to hang out (Granville Island nearly every weekend)
4. The name of the mall closest to her house
5. That she works part-time at the video store
6. And the kicker—SHE'S GOT A FRIEND NAMED CLARICE.

I was all over her when I saw that last one. Practically ready to walk out the door and let her deal with everything on her own. She can have all the panic attacks she wants and I won't care. Hell, she *should* have a panic attack!

When I asked if she mentioned that I work at Child Find, she just looked at me with those scared brown eyes. First she said no, then she said, "I don't think so...I'm sure I didn't. I totally didn't!" Not exactly confidence-building.

When she told me that she'd already quit the video store, I just rolled my eyes at her and said, "Do you think he won't be able to con your address out of one of those dorks who work there?"

Obviously she hadn't given *that* any thought. Honestly, it's like dealing with a five-year-old.

Still, I can't let Shelby get trapped. Aside from her being a friend, the guy knows about me, too.

And what does she know about the creepo?

1. That he was in a jail "somewhere in the prairies." Maybe.
2. He might have lived in Saskatoon at some point. Maybe.
3. His nickname is Turk.
4. He's going to meet up with an old "Roomie" and the Roomie's daughter in Edmonton on his way to L.A.

Once Shelby calmed down, she managed to come up with one semi-practical idea.

"Maybe we can check with some of the pens and see if someone named Turk is getting out soon?"

Fine, if he's not already here in Van looking for her

right now. You should have seen the look on her face when I said that.

Then I suggested that she try writing to him—sounds weird, I know, but that's one sure way of getting some sort of information.

Turns out she hadn't written to him for nearly a week, so we had to make up something about her computer crashing and her parents not letting her use theirs because she's being punished.

After about a million tries, we came up with a believable message. The first couple didn't sound like her old messages and I was afraid the Turkey would be suspicious. But finally she got the right tone. All *not-too-bright-gee-do-you-think-we-could-meet* crap. I had to press "Send" quickly before she chickened out.

In spite of the beer, we didn't get much sleep. Shelby was too freaked. She must have run downstairs ten times just to check if the alarm system was set. You better believe the doors and windows were all locked—I checked that myself when I first got there.

There's something I never mentioned to Shelby. As I was reading through the messages, one bit suddenly hit me. This Turk guy says that his friend, the Roomie who's 'checked out' doesn't really have a daughter. Just some kid he "picked up" at a campground in Northern B.C. It's a chilling bit of information and it stopped me cold. I know it might not mean anything, but now I remember something else.

I wish this wasn't a long weekend. I can't wait to get to my Child Find computer and check up on a few things. I've been wracking my brain but I don't remember anybody being kidnapped from a campground in the last few years. But it could have happened, right? Maybe it wasn't even reported, if the girl was old enough and went willingly. But even if it was a runaway, she should be on our list. And something about the timing involved bothers me.

How long a sentence was this Roomie serving? Turk doesn't mention what he's in for but says the Roomie "did some knife work". That sounds as if there'd be a fairly long sentence, especially if they called it attempted murder. How many years was it since he "picked up" that girl? And the million dollar question I'm not sure I want answered—who is this 'Roomie'?

chapter twenty-one

Leesa

I've decided that the worst part of my week at Friesen's is Sunday nights—just the getting back into it after my lovely day at home. Though Saturday mornings are pretty nasty, too. Rhonda's hangovers have become standard but the thing is, now that I know about the black car, I don't like to keep the kids sitting out on the front lawn.

There's a paddling pool in the backyard and a high fence though, so we have our campouts there. By this Saturday morning we've had two hot days in a row. "Scorchers," Aunt Rosie calls them. And it's looking as if the thermometer's going to go even higher today. Dawson is cranky but he isn't sure why, so Aggie and I are treating him with kid gloves. I'm also trying to make sure he keeps his hat on in the sun but he doesn't want to because it's hot, so that's a constant battle. Aggie's hair is bleached almost white in the sun and I've got it up in a pony tail but the wispy bits bother her, so she's starting to fuss, too.

"It's going to storm tonight," I tell her, hoping to distract her. Aggie likes storms and one thing you learn if you live in this part of Alberta is that after two or three really hot days you're bound to get a killer thunderstorm. I've brought out a couple of sheets of paper and some crayons. If I only let Aggie have one crayon at a time we can keep Dawson from getting into trouble. Besides he's got his pool and I arrange the big umbrella so he's not getting too much sun.

"Why don't you draw the storm?" I hand her a piece of dark paper and the yellow crayon. "You can make lightning with that!"

She's at it immediately. "The lightning," she explains, "is when a giant's shoelaces are on fire."

"And the thunder?" I love this kid's imagination.

"Oh, that's because he feels the fire and he's jumping up and down."

I can't help hugging her—as far as I'm concerned that's way better than Zeus or Thor throwing thunderbolts.

When we go into the house to put Dawson down for his nap Rhonda appears. "While Dawson's sleeping, you and Aggie can go to the store for me. Pick up some wieners and buns—you can give the kids hot dogs for supper."

I don't say anything. It's just a few blocks but it's unbearably hot and we'll be walking most of the way without shade. I'm worried about Aggie getting sunstroke but her mother doesn't seem to care and there's no point in arguing, so I take the money she's handing me and go. I don't mind going myself and I'm tempted to suggest that Aggie stay home, but it's as if she reads my mind and gives me a look that seems to say, "Don't leave me with my grumpy mother!" And so, of course, I don't.

We get there okay and buy everything. Aggie's face is beet red so we take our time, letting her cool off in the air-conditioned store before we set out for home. We're only halfway home when I can see Aggie's having a problem. She's not saying anything or crying, but I can tell the heat is really getting to her. Me, too. The only shade around comes from the small shadow I cast, so we stop and I try to shelter her from the sun for a bit. She's wearing her little cloth sun hat, but that doesn't provide much shade.

"Only another block, Aggie," I say, trying to sound cheerful, "and then we can take the shortcut through the Mitchells' yard and down the alley."

She doesn't complain, just nods, and we set out again. I'm not much use as shade anyway since the sun is almost straight above. We've made it to the Mitchells' when I see the Lexus coming toward us.

I know I shouldn't make Aggie run in the condition she's in but I definitely hurry her now, into the yard. The Mitchells have a nice crabapple tree and we stop there in the shade. I fan her with the flyer that was in our grocery bag. I'm scared she's getting sunstroke so we sit down and I pleat the paper and show her how to fold it into a little fan. I do love this kid. Even though she's wiped out with the heat, she's pleased and happy to be making something with me.

Finally, I figure she's rested and looking a little better and it's safe to set out again. Once we're in the alley we only have a little more than half a block left.

I'm busy thinking of all the things I should say to Rhonda for sending her daughter out on such a hot day when I hear the car. It wasn't even in sight when we came out of the Mitchells' backyard and now it's right beside us. Slowing down—stopping. Then the passenger window rolls down and he's calling, "You two look hot and tired. Why don't I just drive you the rest of the way?"

I'm grateful Aggie's on the inside, away from the car, I can feel the cool air coming out the window and know that it would be good for her to rest and cool off even if we've only got a few houses to go, but all I'm really thinking is to blame myself for not realizing that he would know his way around town well enough to figure out what we were going to do.

"No, thanks!" I try to give my voice that cheerful, without-a-worry-in-the-world tone. Meantime, I hurry poor little Aggie again and the car is moving, purring along right beside us.

He doesn't say anything else, just stops as I open the back gate to let Aggie go through. I can hear the car idling behind us but I don't look back.

When I open the back door and push Aggie inside, she gives me a reproachful look, "We could have ridden in the nice car."

"Aggie," I turn her little red face to look at me. "You must never get in a car with a stranger."

She's really bewildered now, starting to tear up and I realize that I sound angry. "But he's not a stranger! Mummy says that man's your daddy!" And then the tears really do start. Silent tears roll down her cheeks so I decide to postpone the revised "Strangers with Candy" lecture till later.

For now, I just take her up to the bathroom and sponge her until she cools off. Then I sit and read to her until she falls asleep.

The storm starts right after supper when Peter's driving me home. Aggie's giant is really jumping and his burning shoelaces are everywhere.

One great flash of sheet lightning seems to turn the whole world white, and ahead of us I see a black car pulling out of our lane, throwing gravel and speeding away.

Just as we get into the yard, the rain turns to hail. Marble-sized hailstones rattle on the roof of the car. Not good news for the farmers' crops or for Aunt Rosie's garden. Peter pulls the car up as close to the door as he can and I make a dash for it.

"You just missed your father," Aunt Rosie says as I come in. "I told him he'd get caught if he didn't head back to Edmonton soon. Especially if he didn't want hail damage to that fancy car of his!"

She's trying not to look pleased but I can see that she won't be mourning her smashed gladioli too much.

And I'm rather enjoying the mental image I have of him racing through hailstones all the way up to the Yellowhead highway.

"I always did like storms," I tell her. "Popcorn?"

Except I barely get it made before the power goes off. So we sit in the dark, eating popcorn and reciting poetry. Aunt Rosie knows everything Robert W. Service ever wrote, so we go through "The Cremation of Sam McGee" and

"The Shooting of Dan McGrew" and then she moves on to "Sohrab and Rustim" and "Alaska." Aunt Rosie's big on long, narrative poems and I've learned quite a few myself. Before I started school I knew pages and pages of "The Rime of the Ancient Mariner." I thought the little book was about my size and would get her to tell me lines so I could pretend to read. When most other kids were reading, "The sun did not shine, it was too wet to play," I was reciting, "Water, water everywhere…"

Tonight that seems most appropriate.

chapter twenty-two

The downpour has made the dirt road even worse than it normally is. And now this hail isn't helping. He hits a pothole and almost bottoms out. He should have listened to Rosie when she warned him that if it stormed there'd be hail. It's been over twelve years since he's had to worry about stuff like this. So what if it hailed in P.A.? If you're locked up, you hardly notice. And one of the things he didn't give a damn about was the weather forecast.

So now he can hear those hailstones bashing onto the car. They look marble-sized and not only are they making him worry about the damage, but they're making the road slippery. He should slow down, maybe even find a place to park under trees in some abandoned farmyard but he's too mad. Driving really fast feels good, even when the car fishtails and almost hits the ditch on a couple of turns. It's even worse when he gets on the pavement. And he figures the Yellowhead will be just as bad. Maybe he should get a room at a motel in Seba, except the car could be even more damaged sitting parked outside. He shouldn't give a damn but he's kind of fallen out with Stony and the old gang so he's not making the dough he used to. Could have patched things up and wheedled his way back in but he's been counting on the L.A. thing with Turk. Pimping's easier than dealing he figures. And the Triads in Edmonton have been starting to knock some of Stony's boys around. There was the shooting in Little Vietnam, too. Time to move on.

But he has no intention of moving on alone. And that's the problem. Things aren't going the way he planned.

The "fatherly visits" haven't worked out. He thought he might connect with the girl during the week. At first he thought he'd just check out to see if she really was working at Pete Friesen's. She was. And then he spotted Pete's girl. Just the age he likes them. Hair like some of those old-time, platinum-blonde movie stars. Quiet kind of kid. Probably docile. He's seen her with Leesa a couple of times. Thought of going up to the door in hopes of getting invited in, but always thought better of it. She hadn't been exactly thrilled to see him at Rosie's. She'd probably slam the door in his face.

But yesterday the two of them—Leesa and the kid— were actually out alone. He'd been in the Dog Gone Saloon having a brew when he saw them coming out of the store. Perfect. Except Leesa took off with the kid in somebody's yard. He figured they'd gone in the house but then they finally showed up again in the alley. He could have taken them for a ride but Leesa wouldn't get in the car.

So he is going to have to take it easy—and he isn't very good at the sweet-talking con game.

No, the father-daughter bonding thing sure isn't going well.

He's only had the one visit so far and he'd been counting on tonight. He hadn't worried about the storm. He figured if it came he could wheedle Rosie into letting him stay. And everything was going okay. At least she'd fed him supper. Insisting they shouldn't wait for Leesa because she might not be home in time.

Talking about when they were kids. Or at least when he was. Rosie'd always been the one in charge, feeding him, seeing that his clothes were washed, and trying to make him mind—bossing him around all the time.

Then all of a sudden Rosie went all cold and quiet.

"You were a bully..." she said, her eyes getting all blurry. And then she just looked at him like he was some sort of stranger. "Why were you so mean to me?" Next she's mopping at her eyes with a Kleenex. "After Mama died I took care of you as best I could. Quit school and just stayed home...trying to look after you and Papa..."

Her voice trailed off.

He figures she did have it kind of tough. Pop spent more time with the livestock than he did with his kids. Then there was the accident and him in a wheelchair for a year or two until he died.

Things weren't going the way he'd hoped.

"Yeah...well...I was gone by then." Glad to get away

too. After he got kicked out of school, he figured he'd head for the city and get a job. Couldn't wait to shake the dust of the farm off his feet.

Oh boy, was that was the wrong thing to say.

"You could have stayed…worked the farm so we didn't have to rent it out…or got a job here and…" She really got the waterworks on by this point, "…and helped me!"

He was this close to telling her off or clouting her, but instead he just got up and stomped out to the car. He figured she'd feel sorry for nagging him and come after him. He could always count on her feeling sorry for him—"the poor motherless boy"—so he sat in the car for a while, biding his time. Finally, he could see she was being too damn stubborn. And besides it had started to rain— big fat drops coming down hard—so he took off.

Why didn't she call him back?

He's finally out on the Yellowhead and it's still hailing but he's mad at Rosie now. It's her fault he's driving on this crappy night instead of sitting back in the kitchen having another slice of rhubarb-and-raisin pie.

The Lexus is built for speed and usually he loves the sound of the motor—the sound of power. But the tires are slicks and not meant for holding onto a road with this much water on it. Not to mention the ice from the hail. Still, he pulls out to pass a semi and guns it. There's somebody coming but he manages to slip in just ahead of the semi.

He'll outrun the storm. It can't be hailing all the way to Edmonton.

So he didn't stop at the motel in Seba, didn't even slow

down, and then the next thing he realizes is that there's a cop car flashing lights behind him.

"Crap!"

There's a semi coming toward him but he figures he can sneak behind it onto a turn-off and lose the cop. That is, if he's coming after him. Maybe the cop's just on his way to an accident. It's hardly a night for chasing speeders, is it?

He doesn't even brake—doesn't want the brake-lights to show—and starts the turn early. He figures when he gets turned a bit he'll brake and just fishtail into it but the road is even slipperier than he thought and the car just keeps on skidding. He decides not to fight the wheel. He'll do a 360. Except the car goes wide and then it's flipping end to end and he's wondering if it's ever going to land.

chapter twenty-three

Private Journal of Clarice Warren
August 7, 2012

It took a couple of days for Shelby to get a response to her email. Big relief. The guy's still in jail. And now we know when he's getting out. August 12. He's got a bit of time off "for good behaviour," he says. I can't help wondering what constitutes good behaviour for somebody like that. Not stabbing any of his fellow prisoners maybe?

Shelby's still panicking. He says it will take him a few days to "pick up" a car—I suppose that means steal one—and then he'll be on his way to "his Babe."

I pointed out to her that I've read the stuff she wrote him and she shouldn't be surprised that he figures he's going to get a *very* warm welcome.

"But I didn't know he was getting *out*!" Her voice gets painfully shrill when she's upset. "I mean…like…totally… OUT!"

So, this morning, I was already standing outside the

Child Find office when Mrs. H. arrived. I'd spent the last couple of days making lists and plans for when I could get back to work. Once I got back in front of my computer, however, I realized…I was scared of what I might find. That is, what I might NOT find. What if Melissa was the only little girl taken from a campground?

One of the things I'd done when I was cross-referencing the missing children was sort out those who'd obviously been kidnapped and those who were just "lost." No strange car prowling around the neighborhood or nobody reporting them seen with a stranger. I hadn't thought to organize them under the location where they'd disappeared. So I checked every missing child in British Columbia all the way back to Melissa. No other campground disappearances. I sat staring at the computer—shivering. And my memories of that night at the campground shifted again. Why didn't I go after my little sister and make her come back to the tent?

I wish I knew how long Turk had been in jail or more specifically, how long this "Roomie" of his had been. Shelby never bothered to ask. Turk said he was busted for dealing, so we figured it must have been for awhile.

So I spent the week trying to screw up my courage to tell someone. When I first remembered the car lights and realized that Melissa might have actually been kidnapped *for sure*, I thought of telling my dad or the police—well, my dad, who would then tell the police. But it seemed hopeless, and I was afraid that when the truth came out, I would just alienate the one parent who still cares about me. Besides there was nothing concrete to go on before. Now there was. Sort of.

Besides, in less than a week, Shelby was going to have to do something. So far, the possibility of having to share any of the stuff she'd written to the guy with her parents was holding her back. She was trying to figure out how she could just go and live with her grandmother in Victoria without telling anybody at all. Like I've said, Shelby is no rocket scientist.

But I could do something. So I finally told Mrs. H.

I couldn't have picked a better person. She is, after all, the Child Find official. I mean, who else could go to the police and be listened to? She even agreed that we could keep it quiet from my mother until we actually knew something and then let the police handle that.

And that was how I came to meet one of the cutest Mounties outside of the movies. I guess I still have a soft spot for Mounties because of the one who'd been so nice when Melissa disappeared, but I tell you, Justin is a hunk. He's just a constable, fresh out of Mountie school or wherever they go, and so he wasn't in charge of things, but we kind of got shoved onto him for the paperwork and detail stuff which made what I feared would be a terrible ordeal, rather cool. Actually *very* cool.

When we got back to the office, I gave Mrs. H. a big hug. Surprised her. Surprised me too as I am *not* a hugging person. And then I cried. Relief, I guess. I am not a crying person. Anyway, it's great to be able to know that things are out of my hands.

chapter twenty-four

Leesa

We go to bed by the light of an old coal-oil lamp Aunt Rosie keeps for emergencies. It takes EPCOR until nearly ten o'clock the next morning to get the power back on. It doesn't bother us though. The old woodstove may not be a modern appliance but we can make a fire and have our bacon and eggs and coffee. I even make toast over the coals with the old wire toaster.

We don't even realize the telephone line is out, too, until we get to church and Bessie tells us she's been trying to phone us to come for lunch again. During the service Pastor Dobbs announces that there's been a fatal accident out on the Yellowhead—no names until the RCMP notify next-of-kin—but we say a prayer for the family who've lost a loved one anyway.

I'd rather spend the afternoon just relaxing at home but Aunt Rosie likes to visit and I've brought a book to read, so I just curl up in the big easy chair in Bessie's living room while they drink tea and chat after lunch.

We stay so long that Bessie suggests that we might as well have supper and she'll drop me at her son's. The phones are working by then so she phones Peter to let him know he doesn't need to pick me up. I admire Bessie's determination. Obviously she isn't going to let Rhonda push her around too much. But it's good for me, too. The kids will be happy to see their granny and if, by chance, my father decides to come back, I won't be there.

All I have to do is get through the Sunday night with Rhonda.

When Bessie and I arrive, Peter volunteers to help his mum put the kids to bed. This time Rhonda isn't hanging around while I clean up from their supper. She's glued to the TV news. Photos of all the cars that went in the ditch during last night's storm and the fatal accident site just this side of the Jasper Park entrance gate. It isn't exactly storm related—a bull elk wandered out on the highway. Maybe if it hadn't been for the storm, the driver might have been able to avoid it. A family from Manitoba: the driver and his wife killed; two kids in the back seat injured but alive. They're in hospital in Hinton. A couple of other injury accidents. I don't hear the names but Rhonda is out in the kitchen in a flash.

"I guess your dad crashed his car on the way back to Edmonton last night…at least they're saying a man named Weldon from Edmonton was injured."

I don't even wonder how she knows he was here in Tomahawk. Did Peter recognize the car in the flash of lightning and tell her? That's not on my mind just then.

Why is it some people seem to enjoy being the bearers of bad news? At least what they think is bad news.

Good thing my back is to her so she can't see my face because if she did she'd know it isn't bad news as far as I'm concerned. The first thing that pops into my head is Aunt Rosie's quote about the Lord working in "mysterious ways, his wonders to perform." All I can think of is me in church last week asking God to get my dad out of my life. So even though I only asked that he move away or get too busy to bother with me, I feel guilty. But I can't let Rhonda see that either. So I shut the dishwasher door very slowly and then turn trying to show just the right amount of concern on my face.

"They took him to some hospital in Edmonton," Rhonda adds.

"Maybe I should phone Aunt Rosie," I say and walk over to the phone.

For once, Rhonda behaves with a bit of understanding. She watches while I dial the number but leaves when I start to talk.

Aunt Rosie is concerned, I can tell. Relieved that he's alive, though, since I know she's feeling guilty for making him drive back to Edmonton in the storm.

"I should have let him spend the night," she says and I can tell by her voice that there's more to it than that. Did they have a fight? Hard to imagine Aunt Rosie actually throwing him out.

At least I can look forward to a week with no black car lurking around town. So when Rhonda decides that Aggie needs to learn to walk back and forth to kindergarten before September we decide to do a couple of dry runs with me pushing Dawson along in the stroller.

Once again, Tomahawk seems like the safe old town it used to be.

chapter twenty-five

He wakes up in the ambulance with a hell of a headache, and tries to persuade the attendant to give him something for the pain. OxyContin or Percocet, maybe. No luck. The snot-nosed kid posing as an attendant claims they can't. Bloody liar! He's pretty sure they'd have demerol or morphine to give if they really wanted to help somebody.

So he's moaning more than necessary just to make an impression, hoping the guy will relent.

"Where am I?" He means where are they, of course. Whereabouts on the highway. "Where are you taking me?"

The jerk ignores the first question but answers the second. "We're taking you to Emergency at the Misericordia Hospital in Edmonton," he says pronouncing each word slowly as if he's talking to somebody from outer space.

Well, that's something. At least he'll be back in the city.

"My car?" Damn, it's probably totalled and he still

owes Stony on it. Means he'll have to go back to dealing for him. Not good. He's on parole and he's got to watch his back. He scored a few times to get some quick cash, but mostly to people he knew from before. Safe. Now he'll have to take more chances.

This time he's groaning for real. And his head hurts. Pounding like somebody's stuck a jackhammer in there. He tries to sit up and grab the guy but just falls back and fades away again.

Next time he wakes up, they're at the hospital and the ambulance guys are unloading him, bouncing him inside and the bright lights are killing his head. He exaggerates the pain, hoping the doctor will give him a shot. These guys have morphine for sure, don't they? If he's persuasive enough maybe he can get a prescription—sell the stuff on the street after he gets out of here. He keeps on moaning all the time the doctors are examining him. Most of the time it's just his head—shining little lights in his eyes. But they check him all over for broken bones.

No injuries, no sign of internal bleeding, but they're going to keep him overnight on account of a possible concussion. He's okay. At least he won't be hobbling around in a cast when Turk gets to Edmonton. No car though and that's going to be a problem. They may have to stay here for a while until they can get enough for another car. Probably something not so showy this time. Can't afford a late model anyway. He'll blend in better in some old beater. Just good enough to get him back to Tomahawk to pick up his "daughter" and then he'll be out of the country with Turk on the road to L.A.

At last they do give him a shot for the pain. As he drifts away it crosses his mind to hope that the cops don't find the stuff in the car before it's towed away.

chapter twenty-six

Leesa

The week goes by quickly. Funny how, now that I've only got a few weeks left, time is starting to move. I'm going to miss Aggie though and we're already making plans for things to do when I babysit from time to time. She's so excited about starting kindergarten. I've brought her a couple of old scribblers so she can practice printing her ABCs. We don't have to hide those from Rhonda, just keep Dawson from scribbling in them. Not a problem. He's turning into quite a good little kid. Calls me 'Eeesah' like I'm some Old Testament prophet or something. I'll miss him too.

And I guess the blessing of not expecting to see that car everytime I go out or come home is part of why I'm feeling so happy. Aunt Rosie's looking more relaxed, too, and it's not just because we're not so broke. Fall is a good time for us. Even though everybody has a garden here and is giving away tomatoes and cucumbers and other garden stuff, Aunt

Rosie has a stall at the Farmer's Market in Edson and makes some money there. Her currant jelly is a big seller, and my arms and hands are scratched from picking raspberries for her to sell.

She makes the best dill pickles in the county, and when I come home Saturday night, there is brine steaming on the stove. The sharp smell of the vinegar brings tears to my eyes. She's still packing the sterilized jars when I get there, so I help her. Just as I always have.

Then it comes out that she did "sort of" throw my dad out the night of the storm and she's feeling guilty the way a good person like Aunt Rosie would.

"What if he'd been killed?" Her voice is breaking. She's on the verge of tears. "I'd never have been able to forgive myself...my own brother!"

I try to think of something to console her. It won't be enough just to say that he didn't die and leave it at that. "It's not your fault he drives like a maniac," I say. "You should have seen him taking off down the road."

I'm not sure if that's helping much but I don't give up. "It's a wonder he didn't go in the ditch right here."

Aunt Rosie doesn't look too comforted. "If only he had," she says, "he could have walked back here and been safe."

That sends a chill down my spine and though I don't dare say it, I'm grateful that's not the way it happened. I finish tucking the small cucumbers into each jar and then cram in some horseradish leaves. Aunt Rosie claims they keep the pickles green and crunchy. She pours the hot brine into the jars.

"Well, he's okay, isn't he?" I'm not sure I really want to know. I'm pretty sure I don't care but it seems the right thing to say.

"Yes, I phoned the hospital in Edmonton…got the right one on my first try…and they told me he was just shaken up."

"Oh?" I shouldn't be surprised, I guess, but I didn't know she'd done this.

As she fills the jars, I follow along putting on the sealing rings, glass tops, and finally the metal lids. After the pickles have cooled and sealed, one of us will tighten them. We've got the process down to assembly-line efficiency.

"Yes, they were going to keep him in for observation, but there are no broken bones or anything serious." She sounds relieved and her voice is back to normal.

"You know, I really think maybe he's changed…he brought Bonnie a treat every time he came." Aunt Rosie shakes her head as if she can hardly believe it. "And he used to be so mean to our farm dogs…"

"So…" I just want to get away from the whole topic. "Popcorn and a movie?"

It's become our Saturday night ritual. Once DVDs came in, a lot of her friends gave us their old VHS movies, so we've got quite a collection. Tonight's my turn to pick and I choose *The Princess Bride*, which is my personal favourite, again. I've probably seen it a dozen times already, but I don't care. I need something safe and familiar. There's this nagging thought in the back of my mind: even though Aunt Rosie seems to have forgiven herself for "throwing her brother out into the storm" she's going to treat him differently the next time she sees him—welcome him back with open arms or something.

So when it comes to my favourite part of the movie where I usually chime in, "My name is Inigo Montoya. You killed my father—prepare to die!" I don't say a word.

And I don't look at Aunt Rosie either because I'm afraid to see the guilty look back on her face.

chapter twenty-seven

Private Journal of Clarice Warren
August 12, 2012

Maybe I expected something like those TV crime shows where they cram an entire investigation into an hour show, but it seems to me things are going very slowly.

They've had to talk to Shelby and her parents, of course, and she's not speaking to me—or at least she's not *speaking* to me—just yelling. I get nasty texts and frequent phone calls telling me that she'll never trust me again, etc. etc. No good trying to explain that she should be grateful because now the police have identified the Turkey and are keeping an eye on him.

At least I guess they are. Justin talks to me when I phone but he doesn't seem to be able to tell me anything. Apparently Turk has had more than one roommate who's now on the outside and we never did manage to get a name out of him. As soon as Shelby's parents found out about the whole correspondence, she was grounded, watched like a hawk and not allowed anywhere near a computer, so obviously there's been no more communication.

I've tried telling her it's a good thing. That she doesn't want to be alone at home or walking around if the guy shows up.

But then she goes into another of her "You call yourself a friend!" rants and hangs up on me.

Oh, well. I've got Mrs. H. and Justin the Mountie—sort of—to talk to. We managed to persuade Detective Oldham, Justin's boss, that it wasn't a good idea to tell my mother anything yet. I can't imagine what would happen to the Shadow Woman if we got her hopes up and nothing came of it.

Don't know when I started calling her the Shadow Woman or when she stopped being the Organizer type of person she used to be when Melissa first disappeared. I never really noticed the change in her since her attitude to me was always the same. If she noticed me at all, it was as if I was just an obstacle in her way—the little girl in the campground standing with her arms out who was run over. The child she didn't want.

It wasn't until Mrs. Hansen mentioned how my mother hardly ever came to the office any more and barely participated in the meetings when she did attend, that I realized how great the change had been. What happened to that other woman? The one who'd been so determined? Maybe it was the anger that kept her going. Anger at the police but most of all at Dad and me, even though Dad managed to escape. Anger gave her focus somehow. Now she doesn't do anything but watch the soaps on TV as far as I can see, though sometimes when I come home she's just sitting and staring at Melissa's portrait. I used to wish she had a job so she wouldn't be on my case about school. Something that kept her busy and out of the way, like the Child Find volunteering used to do. Now I wish she was working for her own sake—to give her a little outside interest in life. Something. Anything.

This year there wasn't any more phoning, trying to get the media to dredge up the case on the anniversary of Melissa's disappearance. The anger at the media for losing interest is gone. She doesn't even try anymore. She's gone from Angry Crusader to Shadow Woman.

Probably I just appreciated that things were a little more peaceful. And I kept out of her way. I had my life at school. When I started getting into more and more trouble, when there were all those phone calls from the principal, I just assumed that she couldn't be bothered ranting and raving at me anymore.

Thing about a diary is that you get to analyze stuff: your life; the people you know, and especially (at least for me)your own reactions to them.

I guess that's why Ms. Madison gets on at me about keeping this journal. At first, I thought she was just giving me a project to get me out of her hair. The old busywork teacher-technique. She'd be amazed if she saw this.

So, as hard as it is for me to believe, I'm starting to feel a bit of empathy for my mother. Maybe it's Mrs. H.'s influence as well as the journalling (is that even supposed to be a verb?). Sometimes I forget this isn't an assignment and nobody but me is going to notice my mistakes!

And now maybe Justin has something to do with me

feeling more sympathy for her. Before Justin, nobody figured Melissa's disappearance might have been hard on ME. It's the first time anybody's put me first. The first time he asked how I was doing, "coping with everything," my eyes filled with tears. I feel a little guilty because I knew they were tears more for me than for my missing sister—though he wouldn't know that. And he reached out and patted my hand.

The other day, I finally got the courage to go down to the station and see if I could find anything out. Justin brought coffee into the interview room—he seemed pretty happy to see me. Which was nice.

"It seems your friend Shelby's pen-pal has been released from the Prince Albert Penetentiary," he said.

I laughed. "Nice pun," I said. And then added, "PEN-pal, I mean," just in case.

Then he laughed, too, and I felt stupid to have doubted he had a good sense of humour. But his laugh is so warm that we just kept laughing until I got embarrassed and spilt my coffee like a clumsy cow.

But he just laughed some more and used his handkerchief to mop it up.

Before I could feel like a total dweeb, he offered to drop me off at home. "Can't be too careful on the 'mean streets,'" he says.

I knew he was joking since I found my way there on the "mean streets" just fine, but I jumped at the offer and the chance to spend more time with him. I was sort of worried about arriving home in a police car in case I actually had to explain it to my mother—as if she'd notice—but we used one of those unmarked cars detectives use so it didn't matter anyway.

We hardly talked on the way home. (Awkward!) But then when we got to the house, he opened my door for me and walked me to the steps just like an actual date—but minus the wrestling match I have with most of the guys I've dated.

"Drop by the station if you want to talk again," he said with me just looking at those eyes like I'm hypnotized. "Promise!"

So, of course, I promised.

I went inside and actually did a little Happy Dance— and I am *not* the Happy Dancer type. Somehow, I'm going to have to restrain myself from showing up again tomorrow.

Even though I'm not much wiser than I was before, I'm convinced now that one other person really is focusing seriously on Melissa's case. And focusing on me!

Which means now I've got two people who are concerned about me—Justin and Mrs. H.

chapter twenty-eight

Leesa

There's somebody in the house and I'm awake instantly. It's past midnight, still dark. But I hear something. Those squeaky boards in the kitchen. Did Aunt Rosie get up for something? No light shining under my door and she'd turn on a light if she was going downstairs.

I'm lying here but I shouldn't stay. I should get up. Get out of bed. Get away. We don't have prowlers here. And anyway, I know this is no ordinary prowler.

Now I hear the stairs creak. Somebody coming up. Not Aunt Rosie, I know her step. This person is pausing, trying to be quiet. He should know those old stairs but maybe he's forgotten. The only way they don't creak is if you step right on the side—by the wall—and then you have to be careful.

I slip out of bed silently and move away across the room. I know how to do it without making a sound. Lots of practice sneaking down to snitch a brownie or a cookie for a late night snack. Not that Aunt Rosie ever would have minded but it was kind of a game I liked to play when I was younger. Now, by the time my bedroom door creaks open, I am over on the opposite side of the room tucked in beside the big old wardrobe.

He moves slowly, trying to be quiet, over to the bed. There's a bit of a moon shining in my window, faint, but enough for me to make out the shape, now that my eyes are accustomed to the dark.

"Eyes like a cat," Aunt Rosie always says. "Must be all the carrots you eat!"

I fall for her joke every time. "That's *rabbits*," I protest.

I'm glad for my cat-eyes now. I see him move back to the door. Quicker now. For a moment I'm afraid he'll turn on the light, but he doesn't. I can hear him in the hall, opening Aunt Rosie's door. Not trying to be quiet any more.

"Where is she?"

He's probably over by her bed now. Probably shaking her. I have to move fast.

Usually the old rifle is kept way back on the top shelf of Aunt Rosie's bedroom closet, but since the skunk scare she's left it on the back porch, tucked behind the work overalls that we keep for cleaning the barn and other dirty jobs. It will take me awhile to get there.

"Dammit, *where is she?*"

Louder now. I slide down the bannister. It's the quickest, quietest way to get down those creaky stairs and across the kitchen. The back porch door is wide open and I don't stop to wonder how he broke the old lock. I'm back across the kitchen with the gun when I hear the crash.

Now I don't care if the steps squeak because I take them two at a time. The light goes on in Aunt Rosie's bedroom. That means he's moved away from the bed and her. I hope.

He's still talking but it's that soft voice that scared me before and I can't hear what he's saying.

The door is open a foot or two but I can't see Aunt Rosie. I do see him. He's pulling a knife out. And then I cock the gun and move in.

There's an ominous sound of a rifle's double click in the night that scares people, and thank God, it works this time. He looks around, startled. Shocked. So much so, he actually drops the knife.

Aunt Rosie is lying on the floor by the bed. Her arm twisted behind her as if she's fallen out of bed on it. Her face is twisted too—in pain. She's conscious but she hasn't said a word.

I move quickly into the room and around on the other side of the bed. I want to back him away from, not toward, my poor aunt. I don't want him to have a chance to grab her. When he bends a bit as if to pick up the knife, I wave the rifle and move in a little. I don't want to get too close. No way I'm going to let him grab my gun.

"Don't even think about it!" I don't recognize my own voice. It's like the tough gal voice in all the crime movies and TV shows I've ever seen. "Just back right out. Now!"

And he does. To my surprise, he actually does. Maybe it's really true that bullies are cowards. "Slowly!" I order. "And don't try to close the door." I'm getting really gutsy now. "I'm pretty sure this bullet can go right through it."

He looks startled. Scared, as if I've read his mind.

I'm moving after him, keeping my distance.

"Down the stairs!" I order, though I don't have to. He's turned around and got his hands up, and now he's moving down those stairs so fast I have trouble keeping him in sight. He's out the door and I wait until I hear a car start. Not ours—I wouldn't put it past him to steal it—but he's obviously got something better.

Even though all I want to do is turn around and run to Aunt Rosie, I keep the rifle in one hand while I close the back door, take the time to get a table knife and shove it in along the door jamb the way Aunt Rosie did before.

Only then do I run up the stairs. I've still got the rifle but when I get to the top of the stairs I put it on the hall table before I rush into the bedroom.

Aunt Rosie is sitting on the edge of her bed, her right arm cradling her left and I'm kneeling in front of her now.

"Is it broken?" I ask. It's not my gangsta-girl voice any more. It's starting to break and I'm trembling but I've got to hold on long enough to take care of my aunt.

She shakes her head. "I don't think so," she whispers. "I'll be all right." But her voice isn't sure. Isn't Aunt Rosie. And I want to hug her but I'm afraid I'll hurt her arm.

"I'll make you some tea," I say because I can't think of anything else.

But I don't really want to go downstairs alone.

She reaches for me—a one-armed hug. "I'll come too." And I know she doesn't want to be alone either.

Later, in the kitchen, we're sipping hot, extra-sugary tea before she says anything.

"I can't believe you were able to do that!" she says. I can hear there's pride in her voice—but there's something else too.

I know she's wondering if I'd really have pulled the trigger. Would I have been able to kill my own father? I'm wondering that, too. But I can remember the feel of the metal against my finger—tight—ready to tighten. Aiming right at him. I don't know what I'd have done if he'd just stood there. If he'd defied me. Would I have been able to pull the trigger? Probably not.

What scares me is that there's no doubt in my mind what I'd have done if he'd made another move toward Aunt Rosie. I know. And it makes me feel cold and hard inside. I realize what I might have been capable of doing.

I was ready. Ready to destroy a skunk in the chicken-house or a magpie that would hurt my flock.

chapter twenty-nine

Leesa

I can't believe it when Aunt Rosie says we won't call the RCMP. He broke in, didn't he? There's evidence—the torn screen on the window by the back door.

"That's breaking-and-entering!" I say. "And your arm! That's assault, at least."

We're still sitting in the kitchen and it's past two a.m. Aunt Rose is still favouring her arm, although she claims it's just "a little sore."

I'm indignant and angry—and not just because I've been so scared. At last we could be rid of him. "He had a knife. We can get a restraining order or something!"

"He was just worried about you," she says. "He wanted to know where you were and I didn't answer quickly enough."

She can't look me in the eye. "He was always impatient…"

Something about her expression makes me realize that it's hopeless to keep arguing.

"I sent him away…" she murmurs, shaking her head, "…into the storm." There are tears in her eyes now. "He was nearly killed!"

"He had no business doing that to you!" I can't let her get away with that. I'm angry now. Angry at Aunt Rosie for being so trusting, for forgiving so easily. "Just because I wasn't in my room?" I don't want to tell her I was hiding. Let her think I had gone to the bathroom downstairs.

She looks at me, pleading with me to understand.

"He thought something had happened to you. That Peter hadn't brought you home, that he'd taken you somewhere…" She looks down, embarrassed even to admit what my father's accusation had really been.

And I'm speechless. Speechless and furious now. I can't believe anyone could think such a thing. Can't conceive of a mind that operates that way.

She's crying now. "I know. It's ridiculous… Peter Friesen is a man of honour… and I know you wouldn't do anything like that…"

I can't stand to see Aunt Rosie this way. She's always so strong—so spunky. I'm angry that my father would make her feel this way.

"And…and…I was so slow…so startled…that I couldn't manage to get the words out." She finally raises her eyes to look at me. "It was my own fault, Leesa, don't you see?

I'm shaking now but not speechless anymore. "*Your* fault,

Aunt Rosie? Your *fault* that he comes in the middle of the night and breaks into the house? *Your* fault that he drags you out of bed and makes some ridiculous accusation? *Your* fault that he's carrying a knife?"

"Oh," she says with a small shrug, "that…" Like a knife is nothing or at least nothing to care about. "He used to threaten me with a knife all the time before he left home…it didn't mean anything, I'm sure." She doesn't sound so sure to me and I guess she notices I don't believe her so she adds quickly, "He never tried anything with it."

"Why?" I'm not giving in this time. "Because you always did what he wanted?"

I can tell I've hit the spot. She's given up. At least about that.

"He's your father…he was just worried…he doesn't want anything bad happening to you." She has a hopeless look in her eyes now. "You've got to understand, Leesa…It was the same way when we were young. Papa always thought that if I went out with anybody, bad things would happen to me…" I can see she's remembering things I'd never guessed at. "It made him so angry…very angry. So after a while…" she sighs, "after a while I just stayed home."

That stops me. I never really understood before how a wonderful person like Aunt Rosie had never married and had her own family. Now I know. And I sort of understand why she put up with the violence from her brother. Sort of. Did my father get the "mean streak" she told me about from his father? That's what they say happens in abusive families.

I stare at the tea in my cup. It's gone cold but I couldn't

drink it now anyway. Before I can think of anything to say, she's come over and given me a hug.

"Please understand, Leesa…I can't report him. I can't even turn him away. He's family." She sighs and turns to go upstairs. "My own flesh and blood. You can't turn away your own flesh and blood."

And I know she can't. She won't. The next time he calls, it will be as if nothing happened. She'll invite him in as if nothing happened. She won't turn him away any more than she could have turned me away twelve years ago. I'm going to have to accept that. Aunt Rosie is Aunt Rosie and she can't be anything else.

But I can be different. Though I lie in bed a long time wondering just what I can do.

chapter thirty

Private Journal of Clarice Warren
August 19, 2012

Shelby hasn't stopped dumping on me. I turn off my phone at night so I don't get snarly calls in the wee small hours. On the other hand, I still get to wake up to all kinds of nasty text messages on my cell every morning. I just do a one-word reply if I bother to answer at all. Luckily, she doesn't dare phone on the house phone.

On the upside, it does keep me posted as to what's happening Turk-wise. So far, nothing. Zilch. Nada. Of course she doesn't have her computer back yet, so how would she know? Still, I think her parents would tell her if anything was coming through. I expect the cops have been monitoring her accounts, too. Or maybe just the cops. Shelby's mum and dad have never been with it, computer-wise.

Anyway, as far as Shelby knows there's been no word from Turk. He's not coming to Vancouver to kidnap her or whatever he'd planned. And she blames me. Not that I've broken up a lovely romance and her chances of a brilliant future in L.A. with an ex-con. Nothing like that. Now she figures that he never planned to come and it's my fault she's in deep shit with her parents. Thank you very much, Clarice. Never mind that I may have saved her idiot neck. Nope. As far as she's concerned, I'm the reason her life is currently in the toilet.

I don't give a rat's ass. Because even if I've lost my former b.f.f. my life is going just lovely in two other areas.

Work, of course. Mrs. H. is being super-nice and I'm actually sorry that the summer is almost over. But work helped me decide that I'll go to university this fall after all. I'd been accepted to a few places in the spring and sort of picked one out of a hat. The brochure was nice and I figured at least I'd be away from home. My marks were really pretty good. Those calls from the principal were mostly discipline related—that and cutting classes with Shelby. Still, up until recently, I planned on coming up with some excuse not to actually go.

So as it stands, I'm definitely going to Simon Fraser and I'm actually looking forward to it. Marci's helping me pick the good profs for the courses I want. To tell the truth I'm sort of looking forward to it now. And Dad's so over-the-moon pleased, he's actually taking me out and buying me my very own car at the end of the month.

I told Mrs. H. I'd come in and help out when I can. "I'd miss your Nanaimo bars," I told her, in case she thinks I'm turning into a workaholic or getting all needy or something.

And then there's Justin. (I guess that's three good things if we count Dad.)

I know Justin can't tell me too much but he does drop

the odd hint when we meet for coffee. There's really hope they'll find Melissa—I'm sure of it now. I'm positive she's still alive. Justin doesn't say anything, of course, but when I told him about how Mum kept her room exactly as it was, even to the brush with her hair still in it, he asked me if I could bring it in so they could check the DNA. They could have used mine as a relative, of course, but this would be even better. So I think they've figured out which of Turk's roomies they're looking for and they've got a good idea of where Melissa might be. I'm just guessing, of course, and I try not to push Justin for information. I know he feels bad because he can't tell me much. But he does say things like, "If she's been treated like a part of some family, it's going to be a big shock for her...so if that were the case, we'd have to handle this carefully." He's always using that "if that were the case" line, pretending to talk hypothetically, but I'm sure that there's been major progress. I really think the RCMP knows where she is. After all, Justin hinted that she's in a secure home, etc.

So that means that I might actually get to see her soon. I never thought I'd feel this way. Excited? Or maybe just curious? I don't know. Or maybe scared that she'll hate the sister who let her get kidnapped? But Melissa, I want to tell her, I didn't know!

Today we went out for coffee. Not at headquarters either. We sat in a coffee shop nearby. A bit of a greasy-spoon actually but I wouldn't have traded it for some posh French restaurant on the Riviera. Besides, if I spilled my coffee there nobody would care. I could drown in it before the mascara-faced waitress would even notice.

"How do you think your mother will react?" he asked me. "I mean…if it actually happens that we find her in the situation similar to what I mentioned." He looks so cute when he's trying to back-paddle his way out of murky water, like he's told me too much and might go over the falls any minute. "She doesn't have a weak heart or anything?"

A couple of months ago I might have disputed the statement that she even had one, as far as I was concerned, and furthermore I wouldn't have given a shit. So my reaction surprised me. I realized—I'm worried too. After all these years of waiting I'm afraid my mother—especially the Shadow Woman she's become—can't take it.

I asked him how it would all work—they wouldn't just bring Melissa in and say, "here's your lost kid, lady" or something that, would they?

Justin laughed at that. Have I mentioned he has a very nice laugh? The kind where you want to join in and laugh, too, even though you didn't find anything the slightest bit amusing. He said that they'd take everything slowly, probably involve a counsellor to talk to everyone, and then set up some introductory visits with Mum and Dad.

"You, too, of course." And he gave me that melting-eyes look as if I'm something very special. "After all, you're the reason the case would be solved."

So I didn't exactly spill my coffee then, but I still managed to morph into a total moron, since I lost the ability to speak in sentences. At least not in sentences that made the slightest bit of sense.

chapter thirty-one

Something strange is going on.

Turk's back in Edmonton but he's antsy to get out of the country. Says his parole officer has been asking a lot of questions. About Heck. About his "daughter." Says he just wants to head for Coutts and take his chances at the border.

About his big plan with the young chick in Vancouver, Turk said, "Oh, that. Change of plan." Now he's managed to connect with this eighteen-year-old girl with a baby and that will make them just look like a couple of families, so there won't be too many questions. He's got fake I.D.s for everyone, including the girls. Turk's got it all planned.

Heck hasn't bothered to wise him up to the fact that his plans with Leesa have not gone so well. In fact that the last time he saw her it was over the barrel of a gun. The little bitch has obviously got more spunk than he would have imagined. She's not another Rosie, that's for sure.

He'd like to get his hands on her but he's lying low. He's sure Rosie won't call the cops, she never did before, but who knows what the "daughter" will do? And if she tells Pete Friesen, the jerk will put in a report, and with his record he could just end doing time again.

He knows the smart thing to do would be to forget the whole thing and head for the border. Maybe he can pick up some gal with a kid, like Turk's doing. One with a little girl would be nice. He lets himself think about that for a bit.

But then he remembers Leesa acting tough, just because she had a gun. Probably knew how to use it, too. Farm kids did, even Rosie. She wouldn't be so tough without the gun. And she could hardly be hauling a rifle around when she's babysitting. He'd have the element of surprise—she'd never expect him to show up again right away, would she?

He remembers her walking with Pete's kid. Sweet little blond-haired girl. Just the right age. Tender. He could take them both. Couldn't take them across the border, of course. Anyway he's given up the idea of taking Leesa anywhere—all he wants now is revenge. Lots of wild country in these foothills. Caves, abandoned mines— places nobody would look.

He knows Turk's right. The smart thing to do is just cut and run.

Of course he's rarely done the smart thing.

chapter thirty-two

Leesa

It's been a long week. I know that the more days I put off doing something, the worse it will be. The Mounties will wonder why we didn't phone in right away. I keep hoping Aunt Rosie will change her mind—come up with some of that celebrated spunk. I even gave her the famous "Spunk Lecture" she always gave me when I'd complain about being picked on at school. No luck.

Last thing I did before Peter Friesen picked me up Sunday night was to give it one more shot.

"At least tell Bessie…" I pleaded. "Somebody should know." I knew I was playing my last card. "What if he comes back? What if I don't wake up in time? What if he uses the knife this time?"

She just shook her head hopelessly. I know I was making her feel miserable and I feel rotten for doing it, but I was scared. The more I think about it the more frightened I am. I'm not angry anymore, just very, very scared.

"At least if you tell her," I said, "they'll know who killed us!"

As soon as the words were out of my mouth I knew I'd gone too far.

Now Aunt Rosie is angry. At me.

"He's your father," she said. "He would never hurt you... or me! No matter what. How can you even think such a thing?"

So I ended up apologizing but she didn't hug me back when I left.

Now I've got to choose. Do I tell someone and ruin things between me and Aunt Rosie? Or let it be and hope that she's right? That he won't come back and do something worse. These days, I'm praying he won't come back—that he'll just take the hint that I've been getting along fine without him and he can just stay away.

Around Wednesday, I relax and revive a little of the old spunk. "The Lord helps them that help themselves" is one of Aunt Rosie's pet sayings. So maybe I can't go to the police or tell anyone. I can take precautions of my own, can't I? I make plans for how I can fortify the old farmhouse.

The next time I take the kids for a walk, we head for the store and I buy fastener locks for the downstairs windows. Mr. Owen explains to me how to screw them on so that the window can't be pried up from outside. He looks at me kind of strange but doesn't say anything and I don't give him any explanation. I know I'll have to put them on when Aunt Rosie is asleep or out working in the garden. And then I'll have to wait until she's gone to bed to close and lock the windows. It'll mean the house doesn't cool off as much at night, but that's a small price to pay to be able to sleep in peace.

And I'm having trouble sleeping. My nightmares are back.

I've never had one at the Friesens' before but last night I did. Luckily it was the one where I'm lying still, afraid to move, afraid to make a sound, so at least I didn't scream and wake everyone. That would have been hard to explain.

The other precaution I'm taking is to watch for every strange car that goes by. Tomahawk isn't exactly in the middle of things, so there isn't that much through traffic going up to the Yellowhead. There's some, of course. But even the cars from Alder Flats and Lodgepole get to be familiar if you've lived here all your life.

So I'm watching. He won't be driving the fancy black Lexus now. Something else. Maybe late model, maybe not. I'm looking out for other cars, too. I try to remember the sound of his car starting up that night. Definitely nothing as high-powered as the Lexus. Older? Maybe a bit of a beater?

I've got Aggie watching too. Like it's a game when we go for walks. We're playing the License Plate Game but not for different provinces. We look for those with different prefixes that might come from Edmonton rather than from around here. She thinks it's number practice for when she starts kindergarten so she's right on it, very enthusiastic.

Then Thursday night, Peter waits until Rhonda's gone upstairs and catches me in the kitchen.

"My mother says the RCMP were at your place today."

I don't ask how she knew. Maybe Aunt Rosie told her, maybe somebody was driving by. It doesn't take long for the jungle drums to spread the word. For a minute I'm elated. Aunt Rosie did it! I try to keep just the right amount of curiousity on my face—in my voice.

"Really?" I say, "Did Aunt Rosie tell her why?"

He shakes his head. I'm not sure whether that means Aunt Rosie even spoke to Bessie. "No. Mother wondered if it was bad news about someone in your family."

He knows as well as I do that Aunt Rosie and I haven't got any close relatives anywhere. Nobody except my father. Obviously the Mounties were there because of him.

I'd like to think that it was because Aunt Rosie finally decided to report him but in my heart I know it's not true. She wouldn't. She believes he wouldn't really harm us. And she wouldn't betray family.

I know I shouldn't get my hopes up, not even a little, because the let down will be so terrible. I know that, but of course you can't help yourself sometimes. Plummeting hopes are worse than no hope at all. But just before I crash down completely, I remember Peter's words. "...bad news about someone in the family..."

Since there's no other family, I start to wonder. Maybe there's been another accident? So I shoot up a little prayer. I don't want him killed, God, maybe just hurt enough that he'll stay away from me—from us.

So I thank Peter and ask if I can call Aunt Rosie. I want to call right away while Rhonda's still upstairs. I don't want to have her hanging about.

Aunt Rosie answers really quickly.

"No," she says, when I ask if my father's had another accident, trying to keep the hope out of my voice.

"No." She sounds strange. Devastated. I'm used to reading her moods, I think I know every one but this is new. Despair. I've never heard this before.

I keep asking what it is. She doesn't ask how I know the police were there; she just assumes as I do, that everybody in town knows by now.

"We'll talk about it when you get home," she says finally. And then, when I won't give up. "It's about some relatives you didn't know you had."

And her voice is beyond sad.

And then Rhonda is there, so I quickly say good-bye and hang up, and go give the kitchen a final mopping.

Saturday afternoon the Hangover Queen is snarling at all of us so I decide to take Aggie for a walk while Dawson is having his nap. I tell Rhonda it's just another kindergarten dry run but I plan to detour to the store and treat Aggie to an ice cream cone. Anything to avoid the Gorgon-Lady. Not such a bad title either as one look from her and poor Aggie is petrified.

It's lovely, starting to smell like autumn so we go slowly. Aggie picks out a couple of out-of-town cars including one parked in front of the Dog Gone Saloon but they don't look fancy enough for my father to use.

We come out with our cones and start up the street. That's when I realize I left my wallet on the counter. Nobody's going to steal it and I know it will be put away for me but I run back in.

I'm only a minute but Aggie is gone when I come out.

chapter thirty-three

He's just about to leave the Dog Gone Saloon when he sees them coming out of the store so he steps back, watching. Leesa's got the little blond girl, Pete's kid, by the hand. The kid's eating an ice cream cone. He can see the sun glinting on her hair making it look like a kind of halo. It reminds him of the other little girl. The one at the campground.

And then, just like back then, the little one is alone. For some reason Leesa's gone back into the store.

It only takes him a minute to slip out, start the car and back around. Then he's got the car moving along beside the kid. He's afraid Leesa will be back any minute but the kid's moved quite a way down the street.

Still, he's got to take his time so he rolls down his window and calls out. "Nice day for an ice cream!" Friendly. He wishes he knew the kid's name but he's out of luck there. But he does knows a name that will help.

"I thought maybe you and Leesa would like a ride home...
pretty hot to be walking..."

The kid stops and smiles. Then she comes to the
window. "You're Leesa's daddy, aren't you?"

"That's right! Smart girl!" He gives her a big smile and
reaches across to open the door. In the rearview mirror he
sees Leesa coming out of the store. "Why don't I give you
a ride? Cooler in the car." He can see she's hot. There are
damp bits of hair pasted to her cheeks. Moist.

He licks his lips.

She starts to climb in. So slow. He wants to reach over
and grab her, yank her into the car but he holds back. She's
getting in but she's so damn slow. He's trying to keep up
the friendly grin and keep an eye on Leesa, who's spotted
them and is running. "Come on..." he coaxes.

Finally the kid is in and he's got the door closed but
by this time Leesa's caught up and opened the back door.

He starts moving but she's thrown herself into the
back seat, and when he guns it and squeals away the back
door slams.

Now he's got them both.

chapter thirty-four

Private Journal of Clarice Warren
August 22, 2012

Believe it or not my parents and I are headed for someplace in Alberta. Dad's been in the front seat with Justin who's driving and Mum's been in the back seat with me. It's a long drive so I'm typing this on my laptop from the road. Even fabulous scenery gets boring after a while.

We're going to meet with a counsellor at the detachment in Edson and then meet with Melissa. Of course, they'll be talking to her and her "family" as well.

When Justin took me for coffee and told me they'd be doing this, I wasn't surprised. Of course, I'd been sort of in on what was happening. It was a different situation with my parents.

If you'd asked me how my mother would react to the news that her long-lost daughter had been found after over twelve years, I would not have been able to predict it. A few years ago, I'd have known. Ecstatic. No doubt about it. She'd have been out-of-control happy. But like I've said, things have changed and she's not the same. Today she just sat over on the other side of the back seat looking numb. Like a zombie. I keep wanting to snap my fingers and pull her out of her trance.

I did try to talk to her and see if she was okay. I even reached over and tried to take her hand, but she just ignored me.

I guess I might have expected that. Somehow I thought the news would cancel out the Shadow Woman phase and get her back into her old Organizer Mother mode. The way she used to be when she worked to find Melissa before. I thought that now she'd be planning her future, taking over her life. But no. Honestly, I can't tell if she's glad or just in shock.

Dad, on the other hand, looks as if he's just won the lottery but they haven't given him the money yet, so while he's very happy, he's also looking as if he's afraid it might all be a dream. Like he doesn't want to be too disappointed when he wakes up and finds out it isn't true after all. That's him. Happy but guarded.

When we went by to pick him up, he just grabbed me and hugged me as if *I* was the long lost daughter. It's hard to explain but I figure he's regretting that he hasn't seen all that much of me these past few years.

Poor Justin is driving and being bombarded by questions from Dad. Questions he obviously doesn't feel he's authorized to answer in much detail. So his answers are still along the "if that's the case" line although he keeps falling back on his "the people in Edson will be able to explain things much better than I can" response.

Every now and then, I catch his eye in the rearview

mirror and smile just to let him know it's all good. But he's got little frown lines between his eyes, so I know he's worried.

When he came to the house and saw my mother, he was really alarmed but I managed to talk to him after Mum got in.

"She's in shock," I said, though I admit I wasn't sure. "She needs time to come to terms with the whole thing."

I couldn't say much more because by then we'd come around the car and he was opening the door for me to get in. I wanted to hug him but figured it might not be a good idea. Maybe later. I hope.

"She's all right?" It's only the tenth time Dad's asked that but it's one of the questions Justin has no trouble answering, so it erases the worry lines.

"They say she's well and happy," he says.

We stopped in Blue River a while back for gas and something to eat. At first it looked as if Mum was going to refuse to get out of the car, but Dad held open the door and said, "Come along Joanne...you'll need to keep your strength up," and wonder of wonders she actually got out and came. Didn't eat, just had coffee but I considered even that a small triumph. She's still with us. Sort of.

Justin didn't sit with us. Used the excuse that he had some calls to make.

"Nice young man," said Dad. He was trying to get some response from my mother but of course she just sat there, her fingers wrapped around the coffee cup as though she was freezing and it was the only source of warmth.

"Very," I said, thinking, *understatement of the year.* And that was the extent of our conversation.

Justin came in soon after. He didn't look too happy but he didn't say anything.

While Dad was opening the door, letting Mum in the back again, I managed to mumble, "Something's happened, right?" as Justin and I walked around the car. He just nodded as he opened the door for me, but the look on his face said a lot.

Soon after we pulled out onto the highway, he turned on the flashers and it was good-bye speed limit.

"Captain Oldham wants us to meet him in Hinton so we'd better hurry," was all the explanation we got.

But now nobody's talking, not even my father, and I've got a heavy feeling in my chest that there's something bad going down.

Cora Taylor

chapter thirty-five

Leesa

I'm screaming.

"Stop the car! Let us out!" But of course he doesn't pay attention. He's laughing. It's a cold laugh with hurt in it and I know that I've heard it somewhere before. The icy terror of my dreams washes over me. I can't scream now.

He's turned west out of town past the school, but of course it's still summer holidays so there's nobody there. But that's also the direction to our place. For a minute I think—hope—maybe he's going to turn at the next corner and go there, but he keeps driving west.

I can hear Aggie sobbing softly in front of me. I can't see her because I'm right behind her but I haven't done up my seat belt. If I can slide over so that I'm behind him, maybe I can see her, calm her. Worrying about Aggie seems to dull my own frozen fear.

He swerves to miss a pothole and I'm thrown halfway

over to the other side of the car, so I make myself keep sliding.

I'm behind him now. Maybe I'll manage grab him somehow, but for now I want to see Aggie.

Because of where I'm sitting, he's got me straight on in the rear-view mirror. The cold, hard eyes hold me hypnotically.

"Sit back! Do up your seat belt!" he orders.

And I just obey, sliding back in the seat. Eyes held in his snake-like gaze. But I don't do up the seat belt. I let him hear the click but then softly release it so if I want to lunge forward, I can. All I can see of Aggie is the back of her head. She's leaning forward, shoulders shaking, but she isn't making a sound. Having Rhonda for a mother has made her a quiet crier. I want to speak to her but what can I say?

Instead, I continue to stare into the rearview mirror, meeting his eyes. Trying to match the icy look. "Where are you taking us?"

I wonder if maybe the teenaged mother I came from actually lives somewhere nearby. But deep down, I know better. He's not taking us to anyone who'd care about us.

He doesn't answer. But he looks away. I know he's just glancing at the road but somehow I feel a tiny triumph, as if I've won the staring contest.

There's no traffic but then a car is coming toward us. It looks familiar, somebody from one of the farms around here. I try to roll down my window but of course he's locked them so only the driver's control works. Still, I slap on the window, but the guy in the car just smiles and waves back as the car swishes by.

My father is laughing again now. This time I shut my

eyes and don't look at the rearview mirror. I've got to think. I realize that he probably didn't even want Aggie at all. He wanted me. Why would he want Aggie? He just took her because he knew that I wouldn't let her go alone. Maybe I can persuade him to let her go. Drop her by the side of the road near the next farm. No, he'd never do that. She'd tell people what was happening. Wherever he's taking me, she'll have to come, too. And then I remember.

"You know," I say, as calmly as I can. I don't want my voice to sound scared or hard, just making casual conversation. "The RCMP were at Aunt Rosie's today looking for you."

He doesn't respond but I can tell it's news to him and it's scared him a little. For what it's worth, I've got the upper hand for the moment. "They'll know you were in town. I don't suppose anybody in the bar will hesitate to tell them you were there. Somebody will have heard me scream. This car is easy to ID." I stop, look at him hard, and then turn around as if to check for a cop car chasing us with lights flashing any minute. There's a cloud of dust in the distance behind us, but it's more likely just the dust of the car we met a few minutes ago. I know that and so does he. But since I think he might be off-balance, I try a new tack.

"Why don't you let Aggie come in the back with me? She's scared. You don't have to stop—she can climb over the seat, can't you Aggie?" I'm using my calm babysitter voice. Too bad it doesn't work on him.

I realize I've made a mistake. Given him back control of the situation. Nothing to do but just keep looking back as if I know there's a car coming even though the dust is settling and I'm pretty sure it's hopeless. I just want to make him a little nervous—remind him that he doesn't know everything.

Aunt Rosie claims you catch more flies with honey than with vinegar.

"So," I say in my casual, almost-friendly voice, "where *are* we going? No point in keeping it a secret now, is there?"

He doesn't answer right away. I look back a couple more times and then give up. Easy to see there's nobody coming down this road. Nobody on the road but us.

I've just about given up and am wracking my brain for something else to do or say. As long as he's going at this speed it would be insane to open the door and jump out, although if it wasn't for Aggie I'd consider it. But what good would it do her if I'm dead in a ditch—I know he'd just keep going. Taking her. *Where?*

"Ever heard of the Cadomin Caves?" he says suddenly.

Of course, I have. And my heart sinks. I can't trust myself to speak, so I just nod.

The Cadomin Caves are in the mountain above the old coal-mining town of Cadomin. The place is home to half the bats in Alberta in the winter time. In summer, when the bats are out doing their thing, there's nobody there except maybe a few spelunkers. It's a huge network of caves. There are even stories that in the old days, people could make their way through them all the way to Jasper. Never proven. But wild teens used to go there for parties. In the big cavern they called "the Cathedral.".

Chances of there being anyone there in late August are slim. He's going to take back roads all the way, of course, even if it takes longer. If anybody saw us leaving town and notified the police, they'll be looking on the highways, not back here.

Still, if he's going to go all the way to the Coal Branch, he'll have to pass something. He's turning south now. Highway 22, I think. He won't dare go through Drayton Valley, there's a Mountie station there and too many people, but he'll have to pass through Rocky Rapids and Lodgepole. Beyond that I don't know the roads—I've never been to the Coal Branch ghost towns. But Cadomin's not a ghost town; I know that. So there are people there. I've got to contact somebody somehow.

I can see Aggie rubbing her eyes. I'm trying to think of something to distract her, ease her fear. What's in my pockets? A stub of pencil and a little pad of notepaper we were using to write down numbers. I can give it to her so that she can amuse herself drawing. I almost say that but catch myself. I can use the paper. I stare at him as I ease the notepad and pencil out of my pocket. Don't say anything , just stare. I'm so afraid the paper will crackle but it doesn't.

How am I going to write? He'll see me looking down and know I'm up to something. I realize I've got to fool him, even if it means scaring Aggie.

"Please…" I say, letting my voice break. "Please…" I'm sobbing. It isn't hard to fake it, I'm so close anyway.

He ignores me, of course. But now I can put my head down, make my shoulders shake, fake weeping. And write.

Two notes saying the same thing. "Cadomin Cave". And on the back, "KIDNAPPED. Aggie & Leesa." I should use our last names but I don't want to take the space or time. I fold both notes, slip off my left shoe and drop a note in without stopping my fake crying.

"Shut up!" he yells.

We're nearing Rocky Rapids and I figure I'll open the door a bit and drop a shoe out. Of course he's locked the doors, so it'll be tricky to lean forward without him noticing me unlocking it. I'll have to try for a bit of drama.

"You can't do this!" I'm looking at him, my face screwed up, my voice hysterical. "It's kidnapping!"

It's working. He's staring back, furious, and doesn't notice me unlocking the door. I don't give him a chance to say anything.

"I won't let you!" I scream and turn to the door, open it about a foot and drop the shoe. Too bad I've forgotten my seat belt isn't done up. Luckily the momentum of the car helps to pull the door shut again.

I can see Aggie's terrified face turned to me. Poor thing. She must really believe I would abandon her. But I've got to keep up the charade, keep him distracted so he doesn't notice that there's a shoe on the road.

"At least you should stop and let Aggie go at the next town…" I'm making my voice calmer now, as if this would actually be feasible. "It's me you want. She shouldn't have to come along."

He's staring at me, eyes cold. And his laugh is hard and cold, too. "That would be smart, wouldn't it?" He turns to Aggie. "Hey kid…where did I say we are going?"

"A cave…" her voice is soft. She's afraid not to answer.

Afraid not to give the right answer. "A Cado-mine cave."

"That's right!" He's staring at me again. "Smart kid. Such a smart kid would be able to tell the cops all about it."

He's right, of course. And she's even smarter than he knows. I'm pretty sure she could remember the license number and write it down for the police as well. But the ploy worked. He hasn't bothered to look back and notice something new on the road behind us. Will anybody else notice a slightly worn sneaker either? More importantly, would they stop and check inside for a note?

chapter thirty-six

Leesa

Now I wish I'd dropped both sneakers at once. Maybe someone would stop if they thought there was a pair of shoes worth salvaging. Except I'm hoping that I can drop the other near some buildings. I wish I'd done that with the first one. Still, dropping them separately should double the chances of somebody finding them. I hope.

I figure that even if nobody heard me screaming or saw the car take Aggie, Rhonda will have reallized something is wrong by now. We've been driving a long time. I check my watch.

I visualize Rhonda putting Dawson in his car seat and backing out of the driveway, tires screeching. She'll be furious, of course. At me. She'll drive to the kindergarten first and then head downtown. Probably figure out we went to the store. She'll hear about the wallet. How long will it take her to decide to call the police? Maybe somebody saw us get into the car. Surely *somebody* saw us get into the car.

They'll tell her we were taken. I try to remember if there was anybody on the street when I came out of the store. But I can't. I was so focussed on Aggie, nothing else registered.

What if Rhonda thinks we went willingly? For a drive. With anybody else that might make a difference, but Rhonda wouldn't hesitate to call the police on me. For once her nasty nature could work for us.

We've passed Rocky Rapids. My father doesn't even slow down. Not much chance of a speed trap in the middle of the day for people not slowing to 60 km per hour. He's still angry but he'd probably speed anyway. I want to calm him down and most of all, I want to make it up to Aggie for scaring her when I opened the door. I make like I'm checking my pocket and produce the pad and pencil.

"Here," I say, holding it out to Aggie over the back of the seat. "Why don't you draw some pictures?"

He glares at me suspiciously in the rearview mirror but doesn't object.

"Aggie is a very good artist." I am all innocence as I meet his gaze.

He doesn't say anything for a minute. Then looks at her. Her head is bent over the paper and I'm pretty sure she's already drawing castles or princesses. I hope she's not drawing dark, scary caves.

"Good idea," he says finally. Is there a bit of approval in his voice? Is he easing on the speed a little? That might be too much to hope for but I've got to make him think I've resigned myself. That I'm not going to get hysterical or try to jump out of the car again.

chapter thirty-seven

Private Journal of Clarice Warren
August 22, 2012

We're sitting in a waiting room in the RCMP offices in a place called Hinton and I know something's wrong. Dad's pacing up and down like some expectant father and Mum's just sitting, doing her zombie thing. When we first got here, I sat beside her and tried to talk to her about how nice it would be to see Melissa and how I was sure that the person in charge would be seeing us soon. I'm afraid I wasn't too convincing because when I saw the way Justin fled into one of the offices, I knew things were not working as planned. Anyway, she just ignored me so I gave up.

So now nobody's talking and I'm writing this journal entry just for something to do and to keep from adding to the awkward, scary silence. There's enough tension in the room already.

I understood there was going to be a counsellor or somebody to let us know what was going on but so far nobody's showed up. I can't believe they're just going to make us sit here after bringing us all this way. If somebody doesn't do something soon I think my father will have worked up enough momentum to start levitating or something. And now my mother is wringing her hands like Lady Macbeth.

UPDATE

A little while ago, the door finally opened and a flustered-looking young officer appeared. (Not nearly as cute as Justin. Just saying.)

He asked us to follow him into another room and Dad practically trampled the guy to get through the door. Mum just stayed put so I went over and took her arm. She eventually came with me, but without looking at me or acknowledging my touch.

The room we're in now is pretty basic. Two chairs in front of a desk but there's nobody at the desk. I took Mum over to one of the chairs and Dad is sitting in the other so that leaves me to lean against the wall.

At first it looked like we'd been abandoned in waiting mode so I brought out my laptop again. A few minutes later, the door opened and the young Mountie came back, escorting an older man in. From my experience with guidance counsellors, I'd say the man is some kind of psychologist. Definitely not a Mountie. Sort of skinny with greying hair and a goatee. Looks like he's aiming for a textbook shrink look.

Dad hardly waited for the introductions. "We understand that we'll be able to meet with my daughter soon."

The man smiled but his eyes were worried. "I'm sure

that we'll be able to arrange a meeting later today," he said opening a file he brought with him.

I'd like to have heard a little more conviction in his voice. But he stopped talking and just leafed through the file for a while, leaving us hanging. And then the young mountie came back in, handed him a piece of paper, and now we're alone again. Same mode. Dad pacing, Mum numb, and me writing, trying to look as if I'm not scared.

chapter thirty-eight

Leesa

It didn't work. Nothing worked. We're at the Cadomin Caves site and he's parked the car behind some bushes where I don't think anybody can see it from the road. Now he's dragging us up the trail to the entrance. Aggie's quiet but I know she's scared stiff. She actually fell asleep in the car—it was such a long drive and nobody was talking.

I tried dropping the other shoe out as we went by Cadomin but there was no traffic, so all I managed to do was make him mad because I opened the door again.

At first I planned to somehow signal Aggie that if we got loose we should run in opposite directions on the theory that he'd only be able to catch one of us and I'd go slow enough that it would be me. But then I saw him reach over and stroke her hair while she was sleeping.

"Good girl," he said. And I saw the look on his face— like a fox that's just made a kill—and I realized that it wasn't me he wanted in the end. And I remember that voice and the nightmares. So now I know somehow I've got to stay with her. Protect her. Somehow.

I'm strong. Maybe I'm stronger than he reckons. I've been hauling hay bales ever since I could pick them up and heave them into the truck while Aunt Rosie drove it. Last fall, I not only unloaded the truck but then moved every single bale onto the bale elevator we'd borrowed, and while the belt was taking each one up to the loft, I ran up the ladder, caught the bale at the top and stacked it, then ran back down to do the next one. Normally we'd have done that with me at the top stacking and Aunt Rosie at the bottom, but she'd gone to town and it looked like rain, so I wanted to get them under cover.

I'm strong. But strong enough to deal with a man? A man with a knife? There's no doubt in my mind that he intends to leave here without me. He gets a coil of rope out of the trunk before we set out. Aggie doesn't ask but she looks curious.

"It's for tying us together so we don't lose each other in the cave," he says in that soft, sleazy voice. "You'll like the big chamber. There are rock icicles that hang down so it looks like a fairy tale castle."

It was the voice that did it—made me remember. And for a minute I can't move. I just stand there, petrified the way I was that first time at the house. The way I am in my nightmares. Then he yanks at my arm and I know I have to keep moving—have to stay with Aggie no matter what.

Now Aggie's actually running ahead, anxious to see the "fairy tale" stuff. The path's narrow enough so he pushes me ahead. Good. He's not holding my arm but there's no way that I can duck away; the footing isn't that great with all the rocks and scree, especially since I'm now barefoot. I was worried that he'd wonder about that, but I guess he didn't notice what I had on my feet when I ran after the car. Maybe he thinks I was barefoot or wearing flip-flops that fell off as I jumped in when he was driving away.

I can't get by him to run back to the car, and anyway, I can't leave Aggie. So I have to wait. I'll try to keep between him and Aggie. Get her to run and hide.

We're inside now. He hands me a little penlight. He's got the big, heavy flashlight. We're not far into the cave but it's dark already. And cool—cold even. A big change from the outside heat. I guess the cave temperature stays pretty much the same all year round, which explains why the bats can survive the winter temperatures here. I point my little light at the ceiling—no bats now.

"Come on, Aggie," I say, trying to get her away from him and distract her from the cold and dark. A small space in the rocky wall about two feet above the ground catches my eye. "Is that a little tunnel there?" I don't want him close enough to use that rope.

To my surprise, he says, "Yeah, that's what those cave guys call the 'Birthing Canal'. It goes through to a big cave they call 'the Cathedral'. It's a pretty tight squeeze except for skinny guys."

I can see that it would be. But it would be easy for a little girl. I run to Aggie and push her toward it. "Try it Aggie!" I whisper, slipping her the penlight. "Then you can call back and tell me if it's the princess's throne room."

Please Lord, let her go, I pray. Let her hide. Keep her safe.

And then I turn around, trying to delay him. "You must have been here often to know all this stuff." I'm looking up, waving my arms around, like I'm excited about being here. Standing right in the spotlight of his flashlight, hoping Aggie does what I've asked and he doesn't notice right away.

The flattery gets to him and he stops to answer. "Yeah, a few drinking parties back in the day."

I can tell he's coming closer; the beam from the flashlight is blinding. I'm afraid to turn around in case Aggie is still standing there behind me. Afraid to move aside in case he sees she's gone.

Then he's too close. He grabs my arm. "Time to do the rope," he says. "I don't want you getting lost." He's got it looped around my wrist but I still don't try to duck away. If only I had something to hit him with, but I didn't see any loose rocks on the floor when I still had the light.

"Come on, kid…little girl…" He's calling for her, shining the light all around, and I could jump for joy. She's not there. She did it! God bless her.

"Maybe she went back out?" I say. "We're still close enough to the entrance that she could have followed the light and gone out." I rub my arms. "Maybe she was cold…she's not dressed very warm."

But he's not fooled. "No way," he says. He's angry now. "She couldn't have got by me." He curses. "She's gone into the damned canal."

He shines the light onto it but there's no sign of her.

She's had time to get through. I make a dive for the tunnel.

"I'll get her!" I say. Maybe if I can get in there with her, away from him, we can figure out a way to escape.

He yanks on the rope to pull me back, but I'm not stupid. While he was distracted, looking for Aggie, I'd taken the opportunity to loosen the slackened noose and slip it off my hand. Now I'm just holding it to make him think I'm tied. I go in, head first.

"No, really," I say, trying to keep my voice calm. "I'll go first and you come after with the light."

I'm already in the tunnel. Good thing I'm thin and I'm not wearing a jacket because it isn't very big. I'm squeezing through as fast as I can.

"Oh, no you don't!" His voice is angry and he gives a really hard yank this time. But it doesn't do him any good. I'm too far in for him to reach me, so I finally let go. I can't see how close I am to the end of the tunnel, but soon I can feel Aggie grabbing hold of my hands, trying to pull me out. A moment later, I'm dropping out into the big cave.

First thing I do is give Aggie a big hug. "You are the bravest kid in the world," I say.

We can't see much with the penlight, but he's right about this cavern—it's huge, bigger than our little light can cover. In the dark, it's shadowy and scary, and once again I'm impressed by Aggie's bravery.

I know that I've been giving her mixed signals by trying to quell her fear, acting like it's a game. Now I've got to try to change that without making her panic.

"Aggie," I whisper, "you've got to hide. You've got to

sneak out and get back to the car. When he gets through the tunnel, I'll get him away and you slip around behind him in the dark and get out."

I'm trying to hide my own fear and not let her feel me shaking. "He'll hurt you if he catches you…" and then my throat tightens and I can't say any more. I'm remembering too much.

I feel Aggie's head nodding against me. "Okay," she whispers. "I can hide there." She points the penlight over to the side where the cave floor is uneven and in shadow, perfect for a five-year-old to hide if she lies flat.

The light from the big flashlight is now shining in the cave. He's made progress but it's very slow. There's still time enough for me to take her over and make sure that anyone standing at the tunnel entrance won't see her.

"Keep the little flashlight but don't turn it on until you get in the tunnel, and if you can leave it off even then, that will be good."

The light is getting brighter, I can tell he's almost managed to squeeze through. I go and stand as far away as I can in the cavern where the network of caves seems to continue. I want him to see me first when he comes through, but not be able to get at me.

Then I get a break. There are some loose rocks here, not too big to pick up but big enough to use as a weapon.

Change of plan. I grab a rock and run back beside the entrance to the "birthing canal." His head is out and he's put the flashlight down so he can use both hands to pull himself out.

I want to hit him right away but I know that if I do and I can't pull him out of the tunnel, Aggie and I will be trapped here. Maybe the other caves lead to another exit but I don't know if we'd ever find the way.

So I wait. He's got his shoulders out but hasn't picked up the light again. I'd like to kick it out of the way but then he might be able to grab me.

He's shuffling forward, mumbling under his breath. "Where are you, bi—?"

And then I bring the rock down on the back of his head as hard as I can and he slumps forward, sliding out onto the floor of the cave. There's a clink as he falls. I hope that it means the car keys have fallen out of his pocket, but no such luck. I know I'll have to go through his pockets and get them, but I don't want to touch him. What if he moves or moans or—worst of all—comes to and grabs me?

"Come on, Aggie!" But she doesn't. Good little kid. She thinks I'm just distracting him.

"Aggie! It's okay…come on!" But I actually have to go get her.

I keep the big flashlight shining on the entrance to the tunnel and give Aggie a boost up to the entrance, hoping she won't see him lying there below it. But she looks down and I know she does. Still, she doesn't say a word. I hope that now she understands how important it is that she gets out of there fast. Soon she's wriggling back through the tunnel and I'm alone with him.

I take a deep breath and reach out. My hand brushes against his jeans and I pull back as if I'm burned. I can't.

But I think of brave little Aggie in the tunnel and I try again. He's not moving but what if he's just pretending? I look for the rock I hit him with before but I can't see it. He must have fallen on it. The flashlight is heavy though and I hold it like a club with one hand. The other reaches into his pocket. The warmth of him is physically revolting and I'm almost gagging by the time my fingers feel the keys. I pull them out, praying he won't move. He doesn't. No way I'm going to look for the knife. I can't bear the thought of touching him again.

Quickly, I dive into the tunnel, squirming through as fast as I can. It feels like an eternity because I keep expecting hands to grab at my ankles and yank me back, but I tell myself that Aggie will still make it to the car.

"When you get out, Aggie," I'm keeping my voice down, hoping it projects forward and not back, "hide in the bushes by the car until I get there, okay?"

"'Kay, Leesa," comes the little voice ahead.

"Bless you, Aggie," and I pat the little leg crawling ahead of me.

As we progress through the canal, I relax a little. Aggie's out by now.

"Go on," I say. "I'll be right behind you. And I can see her bravely heading for the far exit to the cave. Soon she's framed in the light and I'm out now too. I shine my flashlight back into the tunnel, expecting to see him crawling through, ready to run. Thank God, he's not coming.

I run anyway.

I catch up with Aggie just as she reaches the outside. She's standing blinking in the sunshine and my impulse is to scoop her up and run with her but my feet are hurting on the rocks outside the cave and I know she can make better time than I can.

"Race you to the car," I say and Aggie is off down the path like a golden-haired ball of light.

chapter thirty-nine

Leesa

Every farm kid knows how to drive by the time they're twelve, they say. I guess I'm no exception. Except driving the old farm truck around the barn yard or out in the hay field is a bit different.

"Seat belt!" I say to Aggie, but she's got hers done up before I even get the key in the ignition.

Nothing happens when I turn the key and my heart is pounding in my throat. Will we have to walk out of here? At least he won't have keys to drive after us and run us down. Unless he's got another set hidden somewhere. Aunt Rosie keeps a spare key hidden in a little magnetic box tucked under the fender. We've never had to use it and it's probably so covered with mud and dirt, we couldn't find it if we needed it, but it's there. Maybe he's got one of those. I'm already planning to open the hood and rip out some wires when, on the fifth try, it turns over. Doesn't start, but I'm hopeful. The battery isn't dead. Just so long as I don't flood it or anything. I'm nervous. Trying too hard. And all the time, watching the mouth of the cave, expecting any minute to see him coming out—knife in hand.

I pause and look at Aggie, she's sitting, fingers crossed, not saying a word.

I want to laugh-cry, seeing her. So brave and good. I can't believe any little girl can be so amazing.

Then the car starts and she gives me a smile that makes me feel like I'm going to explode. I know she thinks we're home free. She doesn't know I've never driven an automatic before. But that's got to be easier than driving stick shift, right?

Luckily he's parked the car so we just have to drive around the bushes and straight down the trail—no backing down all that way. If he was planning on a quick getaway, he's done me the favour.

Of course I oversteer at first. I'm used to the old truck. "Arm-strong steering" as Aunt Rosie calls it. This power steering responds instantly. Good thing I'm not backing up.

The trail is long and steep but finally we're at the road. And there's nobody running behind.

So now we have to make a decision: go back to Cadomin or turn and head for Hinton and the Yellowhead.

I pause. What if there's nobody in Cadomin to help or they don't want to help? What if they think we are a couple of runaways in a stolen car?

"My daddy's working in Hinton today," Aggie comments.

She's right. I remember now. He said something at breakfast about doing some work at the pulp mill. We'll probably have a hard time finding him but it makes up my mind. I turn north. Lots of people in Hinton and there are Mounties there.

I'm right.

Just before we get there, there's a road block and Mounties spot the car. I guess they've been looking for it because they're standing back with guns drawn until they see it's just Aggie and me. And we don't have to go looking for Aggie's dad. He's already there.

chapter forty

Leesa

Having Peter Friesen there helps a lot. Aggie's so happy to see him and he can't seem to stop hugging her. It's hard to keep from crying just watching. I'm glad she's got a father who loves her. I find out the Mounties are taking them home to Tomahawk but I have to go with the RCMP to Hinton. I guess they'll need a statement. Aggie breaks away and runs back to where I'm standing, throws her arms around me, and gives me a huge hug.

"You are the best big girl in the whole world!" she says, beaming through her tears. "Maybe we can be pretend sisters."

"And you are the best and bravest little girl in the whole world," I say, getting a few tears in her hair when I hug back. "I like the idea of you being my little sister, too."

And then she's laughing and running back to her dad as if nothing horrible happened. And I'm so glad. Maybe she won't have nightmares over this.

I climb into the police car, sitting in the back seat with a young woman officer. She tells me her name is Karla and I just nod but I don't trust myself to speak. Without Aggie to be strong for I'm shaking—shivering even though the sun is warm—thinking about what could have happened in the cave.

* * *

"We'll take you to Headquarters in Hinton," Karla says. "Your family is there."

"Family" is a funny word to call just Aunt Rosie, I think, but I don't say anything.

I'm still remembering my father coming after us in the cave, and afterwards worrying about him chasing us down the trail and catching us before I could get the car started and drive away. But now that Aggie's safe on her way home and I'm safe on my way to Aunt Rosie, I start to think about him lying there, coming to in the pitch darkness. Or maybe worse, never coming to at all.

So all the time they're driving me the rest of the way to Hinton, all I can think of is—what if he's lying there dead? He never moved of moaned all the time I was digging in his pocket for the keys. What if I killed him? I'm a murderer. I've killed my father. Isn't that worse than just murder? Like breaking two commandments at once?

The drive seems to take forever. I'm grateful that Karla is just sitting there, not asking any questions. She saw I was shivering when we got in the car and found a blanket to wrap around me.

By the time I see Aunt Rosie I'm a total wreck. She's crying and I think she'll stop once we're hugging and she knows I'm okay but she doesn't stop. It's as if someone has died. So then I'm sure I've killed her brother. What if I'm all she has left in the world and I'm a murderer?

Then the police take me away to give a statement and I tell them about the cave and what happened there. I'd wondered about the RCMP having a road block between Cadomin and the Yellowhead Highway. I was sure that someone had found the note in my shoe and called them but it was Rhonda after all. Rhonda and someone from the Dog Gone Saloon who'd seen him driving away with us. Hooray for small towns where everybody knows everybody and what they're up to.

So they send men to the cave and find my father and I'm not a murderer after all. He's conscious and he managed to get out of the cave. He must have felt around for the entrance to the tunnel—after all, it was right next to where I left him. Then once he crawled through, he just followed the faint light to get out. He was wandering around with a bloody head looking for the car when they got there.

I can't wait to finish up here so I can get back to Aunt Rosie and go home and cheer her up. I guess that she's upset because of what her brother did, but I'm just relieved because I figure he'll have to stay away from us now.

"Oh, my poor, lost pet," she says, when I finally get to go back into the room where she's waiting. And she's hugging me and crying as if her heart will break in two.

"It's okay, Aunt Rosie." I want to say, "There, there, my

pet," and make a little joke of it. I'm crying but smiling, too, because I'm happy we're back together. And we're safe and everything is going to be all right from now on.

But then she tells me there are some people I have to meet and we go into another room with a counsellor and Karla. That's when they tell me a story about a little girl named Melissa Warren and I find out I'm not who I think I am.

I won't let go of Aunt Rosie's hand and now I understand why she looked as though she was mourning a death in the family. But I'm not dead and I'm still me and I still love her no matter what my name is supposed to be. So I insist that she come with me when I go to meet the strangers who are my parents.

epilogue

Leesa

I'm still here. In Tomahawk, with Aunt Rosie. So I've got that to be thankful for. But I'm still reeling from the shock of finding out I'm not really Leesa Weldon at all. Suddenly I've got a sister and a mother and a father. Not the father I thought I had—a really nice one.

The worst thing was finding out Aunt Rosie wasn't really Aunt Rosie—at least not the "Aunt" part.

I guess it wasn't very nice of me, but all I could do when I found out was hug her and hang on to her and cry as if my heart would break. Kind of awful for my real family, who had to stand there and watch all this.

And the father I thought I had is back in jail and I don't have to worry about him anymore. I was afraid Aunt Rosie would be worried about him and try to bail him out but she just sighed and said, "I guess he's finally getting what he deserves."

She says I'm still her little girl. Maybe blood isn't thicker than water after all.

But on the "flesh and blood" side, I've got parents and a sister that I have to get to know. The sister is Clarice and she's definitely the easy part. She's fun and we've just eased into things like her telling me what a brat I was, always taking her stuff. So I think she's going to be a good friend, too.

And Dad. I realize that I never actually called Hector Weldon "Dad" but it's easy to call my real father that. He's so nice and kind. His face just lights up whenever he looks at me. It's going to be great having a real father—the kind that cares about you.

Aunt Rosie's pleased about one thing: there's no question I'll get to go to university now. No more worries about money. Clarice is getting a brand new car just for graduating high school! And Dad's so generous to Aunt Rosie—he actually plans to send her money every month. "Retroactive child care payments" he calls them. Of course, Aunt Rosie claims she doesn't want anything, but I can tell she's impressed, especially as it looks as if I can stay with her until I finish high school and then visit whenever I want.

My mother is another matter. Her reaction when we met was worse than mine. She just stood there looking at me as if she was dreaming and was afraid to wake up. Shock, I guess.

"Melissa?" she said finally, her voice soft, sounding frightened and unsure.

I think she wanted me to remember something but it was all too much, too confusing. And hearing my real name didn't seem to matter. Maybe if I could have pretended to be glad to see her it would have helped, but I was still shaky from the cave stuff and then meeting all these strangers who were my real family. All I could do was stand and stare and hang on to Aunt Rosie.

Then my sister, although I didn't think of her that way, came up and put her arm around my mother and sort of held her. It looked awkward to me, not a nice, healthy, Aunt Rosie hug, but I didn't know then that they hardly had an Aunt Rosie type of loving relationship. So when my mother turned and started crying on my sister's shoulder, I didn't understand the look of amazement. Clarice told me all that stuff later. It made me think maybe I was the lucky one.

Sometimes my mother still seems lost, as if she's in some kind of confusing dream. I've learned to call her "Mum" and that makes her happy, I think. Luckily Aunt Rosie stepped in and seems to be doing all the right things. I'm so glad. It seems I'm not the only one who's found a family—Aunt Rosie has, too. And that's the best part.

Private Journal of Clarice Warren
August 29, 2012

No more Journal after this. I found Melissa—at least Justin and I did. But nothing turned out the way anybody expected. Least of all me.

I guess the biggest surprise was my mother's reaction. After all these years of waiting and hoping, she didn't seem happy at all. Just in total shock. Standing there staring at Melissa/Leesa—who actually does look a lot like Hilary Duff—totally stunned and out of it.

I've been thinking about it a lot and I guess it's not so hard to understand really. In spite of making up those aging pictures every year, maybe my mother was still expecting that cuddly two-year-old to come running to her with her arms outstretched yelling, "Mummy!"

What she got was a fifteen-year-old girl looking very, very confused. Scared and unhappy, even. Who could blame her? She had a life and a nice woman who'd looked after her for years and suddenly it looks like it's all over and she's going to have to go and live with some strangers in Vancouver.

I've been trying to figure out how much of my searching had to do with still trying to please my mother. Okay, part of it was realizing that I was sort of responsible for Melissa being kidnapped. What would have happened if I'd gone with her to the tree? Or wakened my parents and told them she was out there? Dad would have seen the light and gone out and everything would have been different. I tried not to think of that but I couldn't help it. So there was a good reason for my getting involved and finally having the courage to go to the RCMP. But the old mother-pleasing desire was there, too, no matter how much I should know better by now. But still, just like when I stood there in the campground with my arms out, I was expecting her to acknowledge me—acknowledge what I'd done. Maybe even thank me. Not a chance. But like I said, she looked as confused and scared as Leesa was.

Maybe it was all the 'journalling' and reflecting back on things, or maybe it was having Mrs. Hansen in my life, but I guess I began to feel sorry for my mother. Anyway I figured it was time to forgive her and stop getting revenge for that little girl she knocked over in the campground. So somehow we've patched things up. Even if she doesn't give me credit for finding Melissa.

Leesa. After all the years of thinking of her as Melissa I'm learning to call her by her new name. Maybe that's a good thing. She's not the chubby rug rat, or the tragic Lost Child or the row of pictures. She's Leesa. My sister. And guess what? We hit it off super-good. Even though I'm a big-city-starting-university-in-another-week-incredibly-cool person, and she's definitely a country-bumpkin type.

She actually informed me that brown eggs come from brown hens as if that is something I could give a shit about. And she's going to high school in a place called Seba Beach. But she's sweet—never thought I'd give a rat's ass about that either—and right from the beginning, well once she got over the shock of finding out she had a sister, she seemed glad to see me.

"You had a doll house…" she said and there was wonder in her voice as if she was remembering an old dream. "…and I took a little chair…and put it in my pocket!"

We both got a little teary then because I remembered that chair. She described it exactly.

Funny, she didn't have any connections like that with my mother or even my dad. Just me.

But now here's the crazy thing. Instead of hauling Leesa back to North Vancouver with her, my mother took Aunt Rosie's invitation to stay in Alberta a few days. And those few days look like they're going to be much longer.

Yeah, I'm calling her Aunt Rosie. Can you believe it? But that woman is kind of like Mrs. Hansen. Welcoming. And kind—very, very kind. So now she's looking after my bewildered mother. The three of them are living in that old farmhouse. And I'm staying with Dad and Marci here in North Vancouver.

I can't imagine my mother managing to live there very long but who knows? She was actually helping Aunt Rosie in the garden. And feeding chickens! Seriously!

To my amazement, she phoned me yesterday to ask me how I was doing and tell me that she and Aunt Rosie were busy making dill pickles to sell at the farmer's market in Edson! And, she's designed labels for all the bottles and jelly jars and she wants to set Aunt Rosie up in business. She's even got Aunt Rosie's friend Bessie-somebody-or-other working for them. So maybe Organizer Woman is back. I hope so, for her sake.

My guess is that Mum will be back home in a month or two and I wouldn't be surprised if Leesa *and* Aunt Rosie came too. There's tons of room in the house. I'd move back in then, I really would. Leesa will definitely need somebody to advise her. Those girls at high school will tear her apart. And she tells me she's never even had a boyfriend.

"I'm a loner," she told me. There was even a bit of pride in her voice. "I am the cat that walks by himself…"

And then she paused as if I was supposed to say something.

"Kipling?" She looked puzzled. "You don't know Kipling? 'I am the cat that walks by himself, and all places are alike to me'?"

So I have to admit that I've never heard of this "cat" but apparently Kipling is one of Aunt Rosie's favourite writers. Okay, maybe Leesa knows some stuff I don't, but I doubt that brown eggs and Kipling are going to be much use when it comes to coping with the crowd at Sentinel High. She will definitely need my advice about how to handle that lot.

Like I said, nothing turned out the way I expected. Who knew there'd be so much media coverage? Okay, I guess I should have figured that out if I'd thought about it at all. A missing girl is found after over twelve years. The kidnapper is arrested. Big story. And reporters fell on my part in it. "Devoted Sister Working at Child Find Tracks Down Lost Sibling." Like that.

Mrs. Hansen said the phone was ringing off the hook. People wanting me to work on their cases! Like I'm some kind of P.I. As if the whole thing wasn't really just luck and Shelby's crazy correspondence with a jailbird.

Justin did try to warn me. Even had their P.R. person give me a few tips.

Too bad nobody gave Shelby any tips. The press were all over her too. "Dangers of Internet Strangers," etc. She actually sold some of the email letters to *The Enquirer*. Of course they had to buy Turk's half as well and so she had creeped-out moments when she realized that if he wanted to find her now, he'd have no problem. Her picture was everywhere.

Looks like he wasn't all that interested though. Maybe he did go to L.A. with his share of the money. Or maybe she wasn't the only silly teen he was corresponding with. Why wouldn't he have had more than one sucker on the line?

Anyway, between Justin and working here, I know what I want to do with my life. So I guess if anybody is living happily ever after it's me. And Melissa. I mean Leesa. At least, I hope so.

Also by Cora Taylor

JULIE

THE DOLL

JULIE'S SECRET

SUMMER OF THE MAD MONK

ON WINGS OF A DRAGON

ON WINGS OF EVIL

GHOST VOYAGES
GHOST VOYAGES II: The Matthew
GHOST VOYAGES III: Endeavour & Resolution
GHOST VOYAGES IV: Champlain & Cartier

ANGELIQUE: The Buffalo Hunt
ANGELIQUE II: The Long Way Home
ANGELIQUE III: Autumn Alone
ANGELIQUE IV: Angel in the Snow

OUT ON THE PRAIRIE

THE DEADLY DANCE

The Spy Who Wasn't There: ADVENTURE IN ISTANBUL
The Spy Who Wasn't There: MURDER IN MEXICO
The Spy Who Wasn't There: CHAOS IN CHINA

VICTORIA CALLIHOO: An Amazing Life